GW00701888

WALDRON

Colonel Tuppen, Montgomery, Eisenhower and Churchill

We have been informed by Mrs S D Scott, who was secretary to Colonel Tuppen of Lions Green Works Ltd, that a photograph of Colonel Tuppen, Winston Churchill, Bernard Montgomery and Dwight D Eisenhower stood on his office mantelpiece until the business was sold. The picture showed the four men walking in the grounds of the Possingworth Hotel.

In view of the connection with 'Exercise Tiger' (see page 113) and the known presence of Montgomery and Eisenhower at Possingworth on 27 and 28 May 1942, as shown by the entries in the Visitors' Book there, it would come as no surprise to learn that Churchill was fully aware of the exercise – but was he there too? The authors would love to know. Similarly, the original Visitors' Book for the Possingworth Hotel (a page of which is reproduced on page 114) has still not come to light. Does anyone know of its whereabouts?

Errata

In the Contents list, *The Last Twenty Years* should be listed as beginning on page 145 and *The Waldron Record 2000* on page 178

The caption to the illustration on page 146 is incorrect. It should read 83 signs, not 183.

Addendum

Even while the book was at the printer, the authors were receiving more information from local Waldron residents and we append two of the discoveries below.

The Thomas Turner connection

There are several references to Waldron in the famous *Diary of Thomas Turner* of East Hoathly, written between 1754 and 1765.

On 24 October 1757 Thomas Turner wrote that he "went down to Jones's, there being a public vestry...It was the unanimous consent of all that was at the vestry, *viz*. Tho. Turner, Joseph Burges, Joseph Fuller, Will Piper, Joseph Durrant and Jer. French, to give to Thomas Daw, upon condition that he should buy the house in the parish of Waldron and which he hath some time been treating for (by reason he then would be an inhabitant of Waldron and clear of our parish, it being a purchase of £55)

Half a ton of iron	£10
1 chaldron coals etc	£ 2
in cash	£ 8
	£20

and find him the sum of £20, which he is to pay interest for; and also for Mr Burges to go tomorrow with him to Mrs Browne's at Pemberry to buy the said house, a fine present for a man that has already about the value of £80."

Thomas Daw was described as having one leg, to be very contrary and his wife was blind. With an increasing family and known to have been a smuggler, he was considered to be a drain on the East Hoathly parishioners who had to provide for him. It was felt that it would be greatly to the benefit of East Hoathly if he could be encouraged to decamp to Waldron.

Very recently the indentures of the Waldron forge have come to light, amongst them that for Thomas Dawe (the correct spelling). It is on display at the Millennium Festival Historical Exhibition 14 – 17 July 2000, and shows that he purchased the Forge at Waldron for £55 on 4 November 1757. This confirms the Turner diary entry.

Just how Thomas Dawe fared with only one leg is not recorded, but his descendants remained in the village for many years as recorded by Kelly's Directories.

WALDRON

PORTRAIT OF A SUSSEX VILLAGE

Susan Russell
Rosalie Parker
Valerie Chidson

including photographs from
the collection of

Barry K. Russell

Tartarus Press

WALDRON - PORTRAIT OF A SUSSEX VILLAGE
First published by Tartarus Press at
5 Birch Terrace, Hanging Birch Lane, Horam, East Sussex, TN21 OPA.
Copyright © Tartarus Press and individual authors.
The photographs reproduced on pages 5-142 and on the dustjacket are largely
from the collection of Barry K. Russell, and are reproduced with his permission.
Photographs of the Waldron Cricket Team 2000 and Waldron Millennium
Festival Committee are reproduced with the permission of Jon Murrell.
The painting reproduced on the front of the dustjacket (artist unknown) is
reproduced by permission of Paul Lefort.
ISBN 1872621 46 5
MM
This edition is limited to 1000 copies
We would like to thank all those people who have kindly allowed us to
reproduce their photographs, volunteered information or have written personal
recollections for use in this book. Special acknowledgement is due to: Mary and
Jack Ashdown, Caroline Atkinson, George Barnes, Beibecke Rare Book and
Manuscript Library: Yale University, Edgar Bowring, Pat Burgess, John
Burtenshaw, Dawn and John Chambers, Di Chapman, Mike and Angela Crowe,
Ron and Joyce Delves, John Dewe, East Sussex Records Office, Doreen and
Mike Farrant, John and Kath Frampton, Beryl and Charles Friend, John and
Margaret Gaston, Yvonne Herbert, Robin Hunnisett, Chris King, Paul LeFort,
Millennium Festival Awards for All, Ian Murray, Peter Newnham, Sir Roger
Neville, Iris Newson, Mark and Beverly Pannett, Jean Paul, Ray Pettit, Doris
Piper, Ted and Ruby Pope, Eva Poulton, Bill Reader, Barry Russell, Olive
Russell, Mary and Martin Rylands, Sister Elizabeth Of The Convent of the
Visitation, Sister Magdalene of Holy Cross Priory, Miss Thurston, Brian
Tompsett, Gloria Tompsett, Dianne Steele, Len Steel, Waldron and Heathfield
Parish Council, Waldron Women's Institute, Wealden District Council, Guy
White

CONTENTS

This book is dedicated to all those men and women of Waldron Parish who fought in the two world wars and subsequent conflicts defending the principles of democracy and freedom of speech, which has allowed our village to live in peace for so long.

INTRODUCTION

This book is a celebration of Waldron; the place, the people who have lived here, and those who live here now. It has been published as part of the Waldron Millennium Festival and is designed to complement the summer 2000 exhibition of Waldron life.

Waldron has existed for well over 1,000 years. The village has rarely been the scene of major events, yet its people have been affected by, and a part of, the seasons' round, the rise and disappearance of industries, changing social structures and national historical events.

In chronicling the village's history, the authors have researched those records which remain with considerable persistence and have come up with a few surprises, as the reader will discover. The early centuries were most difficult to research because of the lack of material, and the first section puts Waldron into its wider Wealden context. The parish of Waldron is discussed in its original, larger form, extending into what is now Heathfield, and including Cross-in-Hand and parts of Horam and Blackboys.

A wealth of material is available for more recent centuries, and the magnificent collection of Waldron memorabilia brought together by Sue and Barry Russell has been the main source for most of the illustrations of the past 100 years. The collection will be displayed during the first weekend of the Waldron Millennium Festival in July 2000, when this book will be launched. For this later period, the boundary has been drawn to include only the area covered by the current electoral register, and excludes Cross-in-Hand.

The present village inhabitants are recorded for posterity in the Waldron

Record 2000, which forms the final section of the book. Even the most modern accounts of Waldron life will themselves become, in time, of historical interest! Waldron is indebted not only to the authors, but to all those who have been kind enough to supply information and help.

Waldron may be, on the whole, a quiet, out of the way village, but it is still subject to the ebb and flow of history, and on occasion has had a role to play in the unfolding of important events. Above all, it demonstrates the unique survival instinct of that quintessential social unit; the village. Take care of it— for its future is in your hands.

EARLY WALDRON TO AD 1800

From prehistoric to Roman times

Early Waldron is often described as literally off the beaten track, half-hidden in the Wealden forest, reached only by winding, unmetalled lanes through the treacherous Wealden clay. Even today, when you do manage to find it, you discover not a village as such, but a picturesque straggle of houses and a church, with a maze of irresistible roads leading you away again, alongside which are more houses, and at every junction a signpost pointing, in all directions it seems, back to Waldron.

In fact Waldron is typical of many parishes in the Weald of Sussex, Kent and Surrey in that its isolated farms, hamlets and dwellings are dispersed over a wide area amongst a tangle of small hedged fields, shaws, woodland and streams. These parishes are a very different kind of settlement from the "traditional" English village, where most houses cluster around a centrally located church. The reasons for this are to be found by looking closely at the kind of countryside in which Waldron is set and at how people have gradually settled here and shaped that landscape over many centuries.

Waldron is located on the southern slopes of the High Weald, where the underlying geology is Wadhurst clay, intermingled with Tunbridge Wells and Ashdown sandstone. Because of its difficult terrain, thick tree cover and not particularly fertile soils, this area was one of the last parts of southern England to become densely settled by people. Historical records show that much of Waldron and its environs was still under woodland until relatively recently.

1

When the church tithes were commuted in 1842, the Tithe Award indicates that around one third of the parish remained tree-covered. A glance at the most recent Ordnance Survey maps will confirm that this is still the case today, although some of the native species of trees have been replaced by coniferous plantations during the twentieth century.

This is not to say that the parish was an entirely wild and unpopulated place. The earliest people to leave a trace of their presence in the area were the nomadic hunting and gathering communities of the mesolithic period (c.10,000BC–3,500BC). Stray finds of their flint weapons and tools show that seasonal hunting parties forayed into the woodland, which would have provided ideal habitat for animals such as deer and wild boar. The earliest Sussex farmers of the neolithic and Bronze Age periods (c.3,500BC–700BC) concentrated mainly on the more easily cultivated, lighter chalk soils of the Downs. Until recently it was thought that the High Weald was largely unpopulated until the twelfth and thirteenth centuries AD, but modern archaeo-environmental research has indicated that a considerable amount of woodland was cleared for cultivation during the Bronze Age (2,000BC–700BC). Occasional finds of ancient domestic objects in the parish, including Bronze Age loom-weights found at Cross-in-Hand, along with flint arrow heads from the Possingworth Estate and a fine hoard of cast bronze axe-heads found in 1856 at Little London Farm, show that people have lived in Waldron and worked the land since these very early times.

So even before the Romans invaded Britain in AD43, Waldron was not completely off the beaten track. In fact, the beaten track ran straight through it. Prehistoric people travelled and traded both locally and over long distances by way of trackways over the higher ground. These formed a communications network across the countryside. The main regional routeways in south-eastern England ran west-east along the Sussex Downs (now the South Downs Way) and the North Downs of Surrey and Kent (now the Pilgrim's Way). These main routes were crossed and linked by a number of north-south running tracks through the Weald. One of these has been identified as running southwards from the Pilgrim's Way just west of modern Wrotham, past four Iron Age hillforts, including High Rocks near Tunbridge Wells, down to Cross-in-Hand. It then continued southwards along what is now Back Lane to Lions Green and then down Dern Lane towards the Sussex Downs and the Channel ports. Also passing through Cross-in-Hand was another important ridgeway running from Uckfield to Rye. Given this strategic importance of Cross-in-Hand, which is also, at around 172 metres above sea level, one of the highest points of the Wealden ridge, it is not unreasonable to suggest that there may have been a crossroads settlement here during prehistoric times.

But, as we have seen, much of Waldron remained uncleared forest, used for hunting and perhaps for the seasonal pasturing of livestock. From the Iron Age (c.700BC–AD43), the Weald attained a new importance, as people began to make more use of its abundant natural resources. Wealden clay is rich in iron ore, and, with the new reliance on iron tools, weapons and domestic hardware, iron smelters began to set up their simple clay furnaces, known as bloomeries. Most smelting would have been carried out close to the spot where the ore was mined, and the large amounts of charcoal needed to fire the bloomeries would have been burnt on the spot. It is likely that many of the finished iron products would have been made close to the bloomeries too, before being traded over a wide area.

The Romans knew the extensive forests of the Weald as Anderida, and continued the exploitation of its resources, perhaps on an even greater scale. Archaeologists have identified several Roman iron smelting sites in the environs of Waldron, including one in Quarry Wood in the north-eastern corner of the parish. It has been suggested that the eastern Weald was under the direct control of the *Classis Britannica*, the Roman Navy, based at south-eastern ports such as Pevensey. This is supported by archaeological investigations of some of the larger Roman bloomeries, such as the example at Beauport Park just north of Hastings, which have unearthed clay tiles stamped with their CL BR symbol. Wealden timber would also have been useful for ship-building.

The medieval period (c. AD 450–1540)

Around the middle of the fifth century AD, the failing Roman urban administration and military finally deserted England. The Saxon mercenary soldiers initially brought here by the Romans, along with growing numbers of new settlers from north-western Europe, gained ascendance over the native Romano-British population. Little evidence has been left around Waldron of the lives of these early, pagan Anglo-Saxons. In Sussex (the county name itself is Anglo-Saxon, meaning "South Saxons"), their extensive cemeteries have been discovered mainly on the Downs, and their settlements seem to have clustered on the chalk too. It is likely, though, that the early Saxons would also have smelted iron, grazed their animals and hunted in the Wealden forests. There would have been small, perhaps temporary or seasonal camps in the forest clearings.

Waldron is a Saxon place name deriving from "weald-aern", meaning "the house in the forest", which implies that there was a Saxon settlement here. From the seventh century, the pagan South Saxons began to convert to Christianity, and built their first, usually wooden, parish churches. Some village historians have suggested that there may have been an early timber church at Waldron, although it is probable that any surviving below-ground remains will have been heavily disturbed by the construction of the later stone church. It is quite likely that the old circular font which now lies in the churchyard beside the north porch, recovered from a nearby farmyard in 1906, would have been used in this earliest church.

The first written records of medieval life in Waldron date from around the time of the Norman invasion (1066). The Domesday Book, compiled in 1086 for King William as a record of the state of the newly-conquered nation and its assets, has thrown some light on the way in which Sussex was organised around this time. Sussex was important to the Norman rulers because it commanded the main routes of communication with Normandy. The county was divided into five, north-south orientated administrative divisions called Rapes. Waldron lay within the Rape of Pevensey which, after the Conquest, was granted by the new king mainly to his half-brother, Robert, Earl of Mortain. Waldron appears in the Domesday Book as "Waldene" and "Waldrene"; the modern spelling of the name was not generally used until the fourteenth century and after.

Archaeologists believe that the earthwork remains known as "the moat", lying in Middle Wood at the bottom of the Cattam, around 500 metres west of the parish church, date from the years just after the Norman Conquest, when the Norman aristocracy were establishing control over the Saxon population. The site was probably a ringwork: a wooden castle constructed on a defended, circular island, surrounded by a deep ditch. This would have had a fairly short-term use as a garrison for troops and perhaps as the residence for the first lord of Waldron manor. One of only two identified in Sussex, the ringwork is nationally rare and is therefore protected by law as an ancient monument.

Much of Waldron at this time remained mainly under uncleared forest or heath, in which the lords of surrounding estates were allowed to hunt and feed their livestock. From the late eleventh century, the manorial system began to

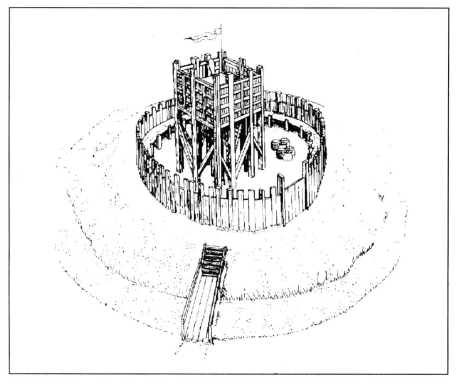

An artist's impression of the ringwork in Middle Wood, as it may have looked when first constructed.

emerge and Waldron, being a large parish, was split between many manorial owners, with outside estates, such as those centred at Isenhurst, Laughton and Chiddingly, along with religious houses, also maintaining some land ownership or rights. Early manor houses in the parish included those at Heronsdale (which historians have identified as the oldest, original manor of Waldron), Old Possingworth, Horeham, and Tanners Manor, all of which today are later, Tudor or Jacobean buildings, probably built to replace much earlier houses. There was also a large area of common land, which remained under the control of the Lord of Pevensey Rape, based at Pevensey Castle. There were extensive rights of common on these lands, and nearby monasteries, including Michelham Priory, Bayham Abbey and Wilmington Priory, were granted grazing rights on them. In 1120, Waldron church, its lands and tithes were granted to St Pancras Priory at Lewes by Robert de Dene and his wife Sybilla, owners of Heronsdale manor, although their successors seem to have retained patronage of the parish priest.

The twelfth and thirteenth centuries were a time of relative prosperity in Waldron, allowing the parish church to be rebuilt in stone. During these years, the nave, chancel, tower and north aisle of the church were constructed. The barn at St George's Vineyard has been dated to the twelfth century and may have been the original tithe barn, in which a tenth of agricultural produce from the parish was levied in order to help maintain the parish priest. Amongst the ordinary villagers, the most common occupation was agricultural work, supplemented by craft, seasonal and small-scale industrial employment, including iron-smelting and forging (at least six medieval bloomeries have been identified so far in Waldron), spinning, weaving and forestry. The large landowning estates of the area often hired casual labourers from the village; the records of Battle Abbey show that, during the thirteenth century, it regularly employed around fifty to sixty workers from Waldron, Heathfield, Framfield and Warbleton in order to help bring in the harvest on its farms at Alciston and Lullington.

The High Weald was at this time considered suitable mainly for the pasturing of cattle, as the land was too rank and damp for sheep or arable farming. Historical records suggest, however, that there has been a windmill at Cross-in-Hand since 1264, which implies that there must have been some cereal grown in the parish. Some of the oldest former farmhouses in the parish date to these centuries, including Dungates, Glaziers Farm and Thunderers on Hanging Birch Lane. These farms would have been associated with the piecemeal, largely unplanned clearance of the woodland for agriculture, resulting in the small, irregular fields which are still prevalent today.

The Black Death, the dreadful plague of 1348, and the less severe plagues which returned throughout the later fourteenth century, reduced the population of England by around one third. Woodland clearance for agriculture virtually ceased in the Weald by the fifteenth century and many farms were left tenantless and abandoned. Because agricultural workers were now harder to come by, feudal ties were loosened as wages rose and the labour market became more mobile. Successful yeomen and gentlemen amassed small empires of private property by shrewd business methods. This increased social mobility could also lead to conflict. The Weald became a byword for lawlessness and discontent during the later medieval period, and the dense woodlands provided a hiding place for many an insurgent or criminal. The unruly craftsmen of the Sussex High Weald were particularly noted for their radicalism and anti-clericalism. Rebels from the Weald were active in the Peasant's Revolt of 1381 and Jack Cade's rebellion of 1450.

The Reformation (c.AD 1540) to 1800

By the end of the medieval period, agriculture was becoming more commercialised; farmers and craft workers were beginning to market their produce in the growing towns. New commercial crops, such as hops and fruit, were introduced during the sixteenth and seventeenth centuries. Most farming was carried out by the family farmers or smallholders, who held their land in a way which required little in the way of feudal obligation, by freehold, copyhold or assart. The ordinary folk of Waldron and the High Weald already enjoyed much more freedom from landlord control than many of their contemporaries elsewhere in the county, leading to a certain independence of outlook for which they are still known today. But despite this, villagers refused to give up their own feudal rights, which allowed them to collect firewood and graze their livestock on commonland, woodland and other open land. A comparatively large area of the parish remained unfenced and thus available to them. It has been calculated that in 1560, of a total 1,230 acres within the ownership of Possingworth Manor, 600 were commonland and 218 heathland.

The population of England doubled between 1520 and 1620, with the result that more people came to live in the parish. Families from overcrowded districts moved in to take advantage of the more lax social controls and sparsely settled land. Squatting and encroachment, the construction of cottages and smallholdings on common or waste land without the permission of the landowner, was reported in the area. Many newcomers earned their living by setting up or working for small manufacturing enterprises. Gloving, tanning, sandstone quarrying, woodworking and especially the trades associated with the iron industry, are some of the activities recorded in Waldron. There was also some poverty and hardship, however, which led to the opening of a village poorhouse during the first half of the seventeenth century.

For at least a century and a half, the Sussex Weald became perhaps the first industrial area in the country. Wealden iron-smelting and working became fully commercialised from the 1490s. The ambitious, entrepreneurial landowners of the area imported the new technology of the blast furnace and water-powered forge from north-eastern France, along with specialised foreign metal workers to run the new enterprises. Blast furnaces used water-powered bellows to heat the iron ore to a high temperature which allowed the molten iron to be tapped off and cast into moulds. Much of this iron was made into tools, building materials and domestic items, but from the 1540s, the first English iron cannon were cast in the Wealden furnaces. This was crucial in freeing the Royal Navy from dependence upon imported armaments. Most of this ordnance was transported to the naval dockyards at Portsmouth and Chatham.

Waldron Furnace, constructed at Furnace Farm on the border with Horam, was in operation by 1560 and remained in use for over 200 years. Owned and operated by the Pelham family during the late sixteenth and seventeenth centuries, it seems to have produced mainly cast shot (cannon balls), pig iron (iron ready for the forge), and, by the eighteenth century, guns. It's records suggest that in 1717 it cast 150 tons of iron. The water-wheel which powered the furnace bellows was driven by a header pond fed by the millstream which still runs southwards down from Little London and through Leopards

Mill, the site of an earlier water-mill, and Huggets Farm on Hanging Birch Lane. The large earthen pond bay, or dam, around 75 metres long and 2.5 metres high, still survives on the northern side of Furnace Lane.

By the 1590s there were sixty blast furnaces and fifty-five forges recorded in the Weald. Several thousand part-time seasonal labourers were employed by the iron enterprises, and many smallholders in the parish must have supplemented their incomes by working in the industry. Most of the Waldron landowning families, particularly the Fullers of Tanners Manor, had interests in iron-working sites, and much of the remaining woodland in the parish was carefully managed as quick-growing coppice in order to produce the enormous amounts of charcoal required by the blast furnaces. It has been estimated that each blast furnace and forge combination required from between 4,000 and 5,000 acres of coppice for perpetual operation.

By the middle of the seventeenth century, however, the industry was in decline. The Weald supported the Parliamentarian side during the Civil War, forcing the Royalists to cultivate new iron suppliers, mainly in the Forest of Dean in Gloucestershire. After the invention of coke-fired furnaces in the early eighteenth century, the industry moved northwards nearer the coal fields.

Waldron played its part in the Weald's continued reputation for radicalism and rebellion. The *Victoria County History of Sussex* suggests that there were armed riots in Waldron during the 1530s and 40s during which new enclosures were destroyed, hedges burnt and animals taken out of pounds. During the reign of the Catholic Queen Mary, a certain Thomas a Rede, a member of John Trewe of Hellingly's "Freewillers" sect, was one of thirty men burnt at Lewes during the 1550s for their strident advocacy of Protestantism. The warrant for Rede's arrest states that, in 1554, he had been "the chief mover of a lewd tumult at Waldron." The Nonconformist Protestant tradition, always strong in the Weald, was well represented in the parish, a fact that did not always go down well with the authorities. The register of Nonconformist meeting places required by the Toleration Act of 1689 records Waldron as having "3 very bad" Baptists.

As land values increased, the eighteenth and nineteenth centuries saw further enclosure of common land and woodland in Waldron by landowners. Laughton Manor's landholdings in the parish were enclosed by a private Act of

Parliament between 1813-18. However, the villagers refused to give up their ancient rights easily. Abraham Baley, steward to the Duke of Newcastle, recorded in his letters how harshly they could be treated by landowners intent on taking full possession of their land:

> January 22 1763: In my walk over the woods I found that the people of Waldron had begun their old practices . . . and this day have sent Ranger to Horsham gaol.
>
> January 31 1763: I have lately caught two others cutting grass to give to their cattle out of the woods felled last year . . . They are very poor and were very submissive . . . I have got a list of about ten poor wretches chiefly women and children that have been pilfering the woods this cold weather and intend having them all before a magistrate at the first proper opportunity and if I can prevail upon the justices to act as they ought shall get several of them whipped, the one man sent to the house of correction but I don't know that anything will be sufficient to keep them honest. They are a parcel of the most distressed and miserable objects I ever saw among the human species.
>
> May 13 1763: I have detected another wood stealer and have obtained an order to pull down his cottage.

In June 1763 Baley was advertising a £50 reward for information on the setting fire to woods in Waldron, and Ranger was still held hostage in Horsham gaol until the Waldron poor were prepared to renounce their firewood gathering. The villagers were forced to maintain Ranger's family while he was in prison, and by October 1764 they were petitioning Baley for his release.

An insight into how Waldron looked during the eighteenth century can be found in a fascinating collection of letters from Benden Sharvell Hassell of Tanners Manor to the Reverend W.J. Humble-Crofts, a former rector of the parish, now archived at the East Sussex Records Office. Writing at the beginning of the twentieth century, Mr Hassell attempts to reconstruct the layout of the village and lists the occupants of each house. Waldron House, enclosed by its wall, had yet to be built. Opposite the Star Inn was an open village green and a pond, and the Old Rectory (a Tudor building demolished

Old Waldron Rectory, as drawn by Tom Gaston.

during the 1850s) was situated to the right of the church path. Other houses also stood on the green. At this time and for many years before and afterwards, Waldron village was known as "Waldron Street".

Mr Hassell takes the reader on a tour around the village, although he warns us that "this imperfect history of Waldron Street must be taken with some salt—as my memory is treacherous, but can be amended . . . Excuse more as it is near midnight! and I generally go to roost at 7."

"The Old House", on the green was occupied by Lieutenant Sharvell R.N. and I. Adams the grocer. In the next house on the same side lived J. Durrant, a Cooper, and then, in the house "of the late H. Eade, lived Jones the Shoemaker". "The house of Jennings and others was built by Stephen Hassell, Mercer and Gentleman." We then cross Waldron Street to Pink Cottage where Captain Walters, the schoolmaster, lived, next door to Dr Stone, surgeon. At the building which later became Daw's Store was a "picturesque Mercers and Wholesale Grocers" run by Harry Hassell. "Mercers—in my grandfathers day were Bankers, Chemists, Tailors, Ironmongers, Jack of all Trades—always

11

educated and mostly gentlemen, associated with the gentry." At "Russells House", (probably Tinkers Cottage), lived Joseph Durrant, "late Mercer and Gentleman." Across the road at the Wheelwrights was John Unstead, "who employed 7 or 8 hands & made superior vehicles—a house now alas!" [Rafters]. "Between it, [Rafters], and the Blacksmiths', [a house?] of very considerable size was owned and occupied by Joseph Fuller, Yeoman." Joseph Dawes, the blacksmith, "was a man of great skill as a farrier in a large way of business."

At the Star Inn lodged R. Haffenden, a shoemaker. He was the "son of Haffenden, Gentleman, of Heathfield" and he used "Akehursts shop as a Shoefactory." The Star Inn was run by William Tester. Next door at "Kenwards Cross Farm" lived "Master Tester". A large magnolia tree stood at the front of this property.

By the end of the eighteenth century, the new turnpike roads, maintained and run by private companies, were beginning to improve communications between the parish and the rest of Sussex. Previously, the parlous state of the Wealden roads had often been commented on. The iron masters had to be forced to contribute to their upkeep by an Act of Parliament in 1585. The main turnpikes running through the parish were those from Lewes to Burwash, opened in 1765, and from Mayfield to Tunbridge Wells, opened in 1767. These intersected at Cross-in-Hand, where there was a paygate and toll house. It is no coincidence that Cross-in-Hand began to expand from this time onwards, eventually becoming a separate, wholly independent settlement in the nineteenth century.

All Saints' Church before 1867, from the south.

ALL SAINTS' PARISH CHURCH

"More picturesque than beautiful, and more remarkable for its situation than its architecture", wrote the Reverend John Ley, rector of Waldron, of All Saints' parish church in 1861. It is hard to argue with his judgement, published in an article on Waldron in the *Sussex Archaeological Collections*, for like many other small parish churches All Saints' has been added to and altered over the centuries, resulting in rather a jumble of architectural styles. Its location, on the highest ground at the heart of the village, is indeed remarkable, though, enjoying extensive views southwards towards the Sussex Downs and over the surrounding houses and countryside. And the fabric of the church is itself not without interest, for it contains many beautiful and historic features which help tell the story of the parish at Christian worship over the last millennium.

Tom Gaston, born in the village in 1882, has written of his own vivid memories of church attendance at the beginning of the twentieth century:

13

All Saints' interior, c.1900.

The services in the parish church during and before the [first world] war were well attended by good congregations. I have known chairs having to be brought in from the rectory for festivals and for the evening service. . . There were more bellringers than bells in the belfry and the choir stalls were full of men and boys making a long procession at the services. Over the east window in the chancel was "Glory to God in the Highest". Over the window on the north side of the chancel was "Let thy Priests be clothed with Righteousness"; and over the window on the south side of the chancel was "Let the saints sing with joy". On the north and south sides of the chancel there were the commandments. These were all taken out of the church and to my thinking it never seemed the same afterwards. My father told me . . . there was a gallery at the end of the nave where the "musickers" used to sit and an old aunt of mine told me they had a base [sic] viol and she said that was music. There was also a gallery at the west end of the north aisle, that being the reason why the window at that end is high . . . I have known what it was to go up to the church of a Sunday. It was a real rest from the hard work of the week before . . .

All Saints' lies within the archdeaconry of Lewes and Hastings and the deanery of Dallington. It is constructed of local sandstone which was probably quarried from Tilsmore Wood. The nave, chancel and tower, dated by their Early English Gothic architecture to around 1190, are the earliest parts of the church, although they have been altered and repaired many times since. Most features of particular interest from this earliest period are to be found in the chancel. The deeply-splayed, lancet (pointed-arched) window set in its northern wall is glazed with the oldest stained glass in the church. This has a beautifully simple pattern, with diagonal quarries of yellow heads of corn and grape vines on a grey background, and has been dated to the fourteenth century. Set in the southern wall are the remains of the piscina, or stone basin, in which the medieval priest would have washed his hands and the chalice during the celebration of Mass. On the opposite wall is an intriguing square recess representing the aumbry, a small cupboard which would have been fitted with wooden doors and in which the chalice and other sacred vessels were locked when not in use. Both of these features have been dated to the end of the twelfth century.

The glass in the Perpendicular/Transition style main eastern window of the sanctuary was inserted during the Victorian restoration of the church, carried out by the architect R.C. Hussey in 1862. It is to be hoped that Mr Hussey took away fond memories of his work at Waldron because he subsequently married the Reverend Ley's sister. On the outside wall it is possible to see, either side of the present window, two, now blocked, twelfth-century lancet windows. These are thought originally to have flanked a larger central lancet window with stained glass depicting a kneeling knight in armour. Almost all of the rest of the stained glass in the church was inserted during the early twentieth century. Hussey's restoration, not to everyone's taste, is thought to have been made necessary by a fire. Features added during this restoration include the south aisle, the pinewood pews (replacing the old oak box pews), the reredos, choir stalls and altar rail. The two old galleries were removed, from where the church band formerly performed, and the organ was installed, although the present console dates from 1903. Tom Gaston's father recounted how the south aisle was built from stone quarried from Tilsmore Wood. This was brought to the church by the Heronsdale carter and his team, and the entrance to the church meadow at the southern end of the churchyard was cut through solid sandstone rock so that the wagons could get up to the church.

The north aisle is in the Early English/Decorated style and is around fifty years later in date than the nave. Reputedly constructed of masonry salvaged from the dismantled chapel of ease at Heronsdale around the middle of the thirteenth century, it is unusually wide, with a later, fifteenth-century roof. Early illustrations suggest that before the mid-nineteenth century the roof was capped with Horsham stone slates. Inside, set in the eastern wall, is an original statue niche, although the medieval statue, probably of a saint, is no longer *in situ*. On the northern wall is a splendid grey and white marble monument in the Neoclassical style, commemorating Major John Fuller who died in 1722. Moved from its original position during the Victorian restoration of the church, the monument is much admired in the Penguin *Buildings of England* volume on Sussex as, for its time, "a very up-to-date and metropolitan piece." The eastern end of the north aisle has been converted into a memorial chapel dedicated to the memory of Miss Una Humble-Crofts, who died in 1957. Miss Humble-Crofts was the much respected daughter of former rector of the parish, the Reverend Humble-Crofts. The old stone altar top with its decoration of five incised Greek crosses was placed here after being found under the floor of the chancel during the laying of its tiled floor (a memorial to the Reverend Ley) in the 1880s. It may well be the original church altar, which was probably removed at the time of the Reformation. Set on two octagonal Victorian pillars, the altar stone was lowered to facilitate the erection of the twentieth-century war memorial panels, paid for by donations from parishioners, on the wall above in 1949.

The present square, Norman-style, font was provided by the daughter of the Reverend Sir Henry Poole, Rector of Waldron from 1784 to 1821. This is reputedly a replica of an old font, the broken pieces of which were discovered built into a wall of the church. There is a story that the circular Saxon font, placed outside the church porch in 1983, was taken out of the church and rolled down the hill by Cromwell's soldiers in the seventeenth century. There may be more than a grain of truth in this as, at the time of its rediscovery in 1906, it was being used as a cattle trough at Dengates Farm.

Although the low, square, western tower seems also to have been part of the first building of the church, many of its best features, such as the battlements, the west-facing door and window, and the projecting staircase turret were later additions in the Perpendicular style, probably dating to the late fourteenth or fifteenth centuries. Hung in the tower are eight bells, five of which are later than 1724, in which year the *Church Warden's Presentment* records only three. The bells were rehung in 1987 and recast in 1887 and 1912. The parish magazine of April 1890 explained their importance:

> Waldron has always been noted for its bell ringing. Out of the 1,013 church and public bells in the County of Sussex there are only 18 peals of 8 bells and our Parish Church has one of them. . . On Saturday, March 15th, eight members of the Waldron Society of Change Ringers rang a true and complete peal of Grandsire Triples—Reve's Variations of Holt's ten-part peal, consisting of 5,040 changes, on the bells of the Parish Church, in 3 hours and 1 minute. The Ringers were A. Dawes, 1; H. Rann (Conductor), 2; G. Ades, 3; A. Reed, 4; J. Beal, 5; J. Burgess, 6; B. Hobbs, 7; E. Unstead, 8; all of whom, with the exception of the Conductor, thus ringing their first peal.

All Saints' church and lych-gate.

An old sundial, thought to have been mounted originally on the church tower by an iron fixing (still in place) was found in the garden of the Old Rectory during the nineteenth century. It is now housed in the Castle Museum in Lewes. The tower clock was donated by the Huth family of Possingworth Park in 1912. The Huths also provided the fine lych-gate at the entrance to the churchyard. Its grapevine carvings complement the design of the early stained glass within the church.

Set into the floor of the nave and ranging round the interior walls are a number of memorial stones and monuments dedicated to members of some of the most important families in the parish: the Fullers, Dykes, Offleys and Dalrymples. The two, large lozenge-shaped wooden hatchments hung in the tower are thought to date to the eighteenth century. Although rather faded, each bears a coat of arms of the Dalrymple family. Memorials to many former rectors are also to be found throughout the church; the names of all previous rectors of Waldron are listed in the church, from Bartholomew in 1195.

Many generations of parish families can be traced on the gravestones in the churchyard, and many of the headstones have interesting inscriptions or picturesque designs. Of particular note is the table tomb of the Cornwall family, situated just to the left of the brick path which leads up from the lych-gate to the north porch. This is decorated with terracotta rosettes made by the much admired craftsman, Jonathan Harmer of Old Heathfield, and dates to around 1824.

Waldron is an unusual parish in that it has two Church of England churches: All Saints' and St Bartholomew's at Cross-in-Hand. St Bartholomew's came to be as a result of the 1862 restoration of All Saints'. The parish church had to be closed for several months while the building work was in progress and during this time services were held in a temporary building at Cross-in-Hand. The services were so well attended by the inhabitants of that hamlet that a wealthy resident, Mr J. Boucher, offered to build a church at his own expense on land at the edge of the woods adjoining his home, Heatherden House. The newly-built chapel of ease was consecrated on 24th August 1863 (St Bartholomew's Day), by the then Bishop of Chichester, Dr Gilbert.

Waldron Voluntary Primary School, c.1903.

SCHOOLING IN WALDRON

Early attempts to "improve" the ordinary parishioners of Waldron included the setting up of a charity school in 1713. This establishment seems to have fallen out of use by 1786, when a Sunday School was begun, funded by the local gentry. The first master was John Waters, also appointed manager of the village workhouse. In a letter to the *Sussex Weekly Advertiser* of 11th February 1788, an anonymous Waldron correspondent explained the purpose of the school, which was:

> . . . to rescue the children of the poor from ignorance, idleness, and vice, and to instruct them in the duties of morality and religion . . . to lead them, by pious and moral conduct, to happiness on earth, and to ever-lasting glory and felicity in the world to come. . .

The school was a remarkable success, as children attended in numbers unprecedented in any other Sussex parish. After only two years, there were 134 children on its roll, both boys and girls aged from seven to sixteen, of whom more than 100 were in attendance on any one Sunday. This in a parish where the total population was around 750. Fifteen to twenty children were also sent to a local day-school. The same Waldron correspondent defended the school against doubters:

> As to that specious objection which some have made, that young persons instructed but one day in seven are not likely even to learn to read, I am happy to have it in my power to lay a-side, as futile and fallacious; for I aver there are at this time several at our Sunday-school, that did not know so much as the letters when they first entered, who are now able to read decently, and without any other assistance.

The school was judged to have benefited the whole parish:

> Our Sunday-school has not only been the means of instructing the children to read, and giving them an idea of Morality and Religion, but even their parents, who before were too apt to spend the sabbath in sloth and idleness, and sometimes in riot and intemperance, have since the commencement of this laudable institution, been pretty regular in their attendance at public worship.

Other early attempts to provide an education for the village children included a dame school run from Tinkers Cottage, opposite the blacksmith's forge. The *Waldron Women's Institute Scrapbook* of 1953 mentions a former pupil of the school who often told how she found the restive horses waiting at the smith's opposite far more interesting than the lessons!

The founding of the first National school in 1854 was beset by teething troubles. Funds were short, there were problems in purchasing the land necessary for the new school building, staff were hard to recruit and many parents could not afford the fees charged. It was also difficult to develop good attendance amongst the children when their parents needed their help on the land or at home. Children often had to take time off in summer for harvesting and hop-picking; this was eventually formalised in the long summer holiday still taken today. The children also invariably stayed away from school if there was a cricket or stoolball match or if the fair had arrived in the village. School records show that age-old annual customs, such as collecting money for bonfire night, carrying flowers around the village on May Day and celebrating Harvest Home, were given as reasons for children missing school sessions. During the second half of the nineteenth century the school was often closed as a result of outbreaks of contagious diseases such as scarlet fever, diptheria or measles.

Tom Gaston has written of his difficult journey to and from school:

It was from the old cottage in the lane [now a bridle path between Foxhunt and Lions Green] called Bennets Cottage that I started school early in 1888. We had to go down to the river where there was a stile. A footpath lead across the field to Tanyard. It was no joke having to find our way through the fields on dark nights and it was often very muddy.

Evening classes for adults were also begun at this time. They were taught to read and write and evening lectures were given. In 1889, two lectures on church history were accompanied by "illustrations thrown by coloured slides from a powereful majic lantern."

Despite the early problems, the examination of the school by Her Majesty's Inspectorate showed that every child invariably passed its "standard". In 1889, an inspector remarked that "The children sung well. Their written work was intelligent and praiseworthy and it is clear that Mr Theakstone has taught his pupils admirably." There was rarely a failure at reading which meant that as soon as a pupil reached the required standard they could leave school.

As well as learning their lessons, the children were given Christmas parties with games and presents and also a summer treat. A typical treat was for the children to assemble at one of the large houses in the parish and with flags and bannerets flying proceed down the drive to where tea and games had been arranged. The chief attraction would be a steam-driven roundabout. A cricket match was usually held between the boys from Waldron and Cross-in-Hand and presents were given to each child. There were usually around 250 children at these parties. Outings to Eastbourne on the train from Waldron and Horeham Road railway station were also arranged. After one such outing, "Mr Kenward

Waldron Boy Scouts, c.1905.

most kindly sent a colossal wagon to meet the evening train and convey the wearied little ones home." The children were encouraged to join the Girls Friendly Society, the Boy Scouts, the choir, the boys cricket club or the stoolball club.

Concerts were held in the school, with singing, instrumentals and recitations. Unfortunately, at one gathering, a few members of the audience talked so loudly that many people were prevented from hearing and enjoying the performance. The school records noted that if it happened again the cheap threepenny seats would be discontinued!

In 1890 an attempt was made to offer inexpensive dinners to the children at a halfpenny a meal. This consisted of a basin of hot soup and a piece of bread. Money was raised at school concerts for the purchase of the vegetables. Unfortunately, the dinner service could not be sustained for long and parents had once again to provide a packed lunch.

From 1st September 1891 the parish school was free to all, and charges were no longer made for books and stationery. One noticeable result was that attendance became much more regular. Waldron chose to become a voluntary

Waldron School stoolball team in the 1920s.

primary school, giving religious instruction to its pupils, and as a result received less direct government funding.

In 1903 the first managers' meeting was held. The headmaster and his wife, Mr and Mrs Bannister, applied for an increase in their wages, which they received. However, a year later the county council took direct control of teacher's salaries and promptly reduced the headmaster's pay by £20 per annum. Mr Bannister was obviously upset and a few weeks later he furnished the committee with a bill for 2s 6d for sweeping the school house chimney. "This was rejected unanimously and returned to Mr Bannister post haste."

Improvements were made to the school building at this time. Hooks were hung in the cloakrooms and hand basins were provided, along with doors for the toilets. A few years later the playground was covered with flint chippings and the pathways were bricked over.

Robin Hunnisett remembers starting school at Waldron in 1932. His father would push him in a handcart from his home in Warren Lane down to the

Gardening at Waldron School.

village. The handcart belonged to his grandfather's business, Benji Edwards & Son, local builders. Robin remembers three classrooms with brick floors, no electricity, no running water and no adequate heating. It was a somewhat dark and cold place.

Many children from the village were dressed in well-patched and altered "hand-me-downs" which usually did not fit. These clothes were often the subject of ridicule, to which the stock retort was "It's clean and I ain't pinched it!"

During Robin's first months at school, slates and chalks were used for writing, as were small sand trays. Letters and numerals were traced in the sand with a finger and mistakes were erased with a quick shake of the tray. All elementary subjects were taught and scripture lessons, taken by the Reverend Stephenson, were still an important part of the curriculum. Stephenson was popular with the children and could often be seen walking down the street with a small child on his shoulders.

Robin remembers the caretaker filling a bucket of water from the well each day for drinking water, while water for washing was collected from the water butts and tipped into small enamel basins. He recalls playing rounders, cricket and shinty—a game much like hockey, played by both boys and girls. This was a "vicious game", utilising a wooden ball approximately three and a half inches in diameter, hit with much gusto using home-crafted ash sticks. These games were played on the Cattam recreation ground, where the children also worked the vegetable gardens on the allotments.

The "eleven plus" was taken, but the pupils made little effort to pass the exam. Entry to grammar school would have meant a long journey to and from Lewes each day, with the added expense of a uniform and books. Robin, like most village children, left school at the age of fourteen.

Over the following years the school flourished and remained the centre of village life. The playground was tarmacked, flush toilets were installed and a proper canteen was provided. The children worked the school garden for many years and trips were made to neighbouring schools for sports and musical events. With the Cattam on which to play sports, the weekly service at All Saints' and the fields and woods for nature walks, the village school provided a

A school group in the early 1960s.

25

One of the last pictures taken, with Mrs Felix, headmistress, and Mrs Gorringe, cook.

pleasant and worthy educational foundation for the children.

However, with the mechanisation of agriculture after World War Two, the number of farm workers with families living in the village decreased as young men were forced to move away in order to find employment. From the 1950s, the school roll fell to around fifty pupils. Nevertheless, the school celebrated its 100th birthday with a party and a large cake made by the school cook, Mrs Leeves. By the 1960s, with pupil numbers declining still further, talks were being held regarding the closure of the school. Mrs Gifford and Miss Jenner were two of the last full-time headmistresses. Miss Truby, another well respected teacher, cycled every day for many years from her home in Framfield to Waldron. Mrs Di Chapman, the school secretary, and Mrs Gorringe, the school cook, petitioned hard to keep the school open but with only sixteen children due to attend the new school year, the school eventually bowed to the inevitable and closed in 1969. The last caretakers were Muriel and Ray Pettit: Ray had attended the school, as had his mother and his own six daughters.

Ironically, at the beginning of the twenty-first century, there are again enough children living in Waldron to support a village primary school.

The Star Inn, with post office, c.1950.

HISTORIC BUILDINGS & FAMILIES

The Star Inn

The present Star Inn dates from the sixteenth century and, although it has been extended and modernised over the years, it still retains much of its original charm and character. It may have replaced an earlier hostelry on the same spot; an ideal location at the road junction in the centre of the village, opposite the ancient parish church.

Traditionally, an inn was more than an ale house; it also provided accommodation for travellers and stabling for their horses. Before the present licensees, Con and Paul Lefort, carried out their modernisation works, the old cobbled single-storey extension on the left-hand side of The Star was always referred to as the Old Stables. Former Waldron resident Ray Pettit remembers the stables being used in the 1920s by workmen when some of the smaller lanes were being made up for the first time. Mr Hemsley, whose horse drew the

The old fireplace at The Star Inn.

water-carrier at that time, used to stable his horse at The Star as well as bedding down there himself. During the twentieth century, the Old Stables also housed a butcher's shop, post office, library and even for a short while a youth club.

As you enter the pub, on the right-hand side of the main bar is the original fireplace. Before the canopy was added this opened up directly to the sky. The original spit can still be seen, as can the old iron fireback of 1694, cast locally at Tanners Furnace. This is decorated with the initials of Thomas and Mary Manser, licensees during the seventeenth century. In the 1830s William Tester was landlord; his ancestors can be traced back in Waldron to the 1500s, and his descendants still live in the parish today.

During the 1940s and 50s, Mr Albert and Mrs Kathleen Smith ran the pub, the library and the post office from the building. Mrs Smith continued to run the businesses after the death of her husband. The *Southern Weekly News* of 1954 quotes her claim, "If anybody wants a postal order and a pint at the same time, then it is just too bad!"

The pub has been used for many village meetings and functions over the years, especially prior to the building of the Lucas Memorial Hall. The village cricket team traditionally had their teas provided for them in the pub. In the 1930s, Mrs Oliver the licensee supplied the tea and Tom Barton pushed the food and tea urn through the village and down to the Hall in a wheelbarrow.

The family of Con and Paul Lefort have been in residence since 1982 and now run a freehouse. Some organisations still hold their meetings in the pub, and it even has its own occasional cricket team, "The Rats" (Star spelt backwards).

Heronsdale Manor

Heronsdale is probably the oldest manor in Waldron, and was referred to as simply the "Manor of Walderne" in early documents. The Domesday Book of 1086 records that Ansfrid lived in the Court of Walderne. His descendant Robert de Dene owned the manor in 1121 when he and his wife Sybilla granted the "Church of Walderne with some lands and tithes" to the Cluniac Priory of St Pancras at Southover in Lewes.

Heronsdale just after the turn of the twentieth century.

The name Heronsdale derives from Robert de Dene's heir, his great great granddaughter Sybilla, who married a Nicholas Heringod. The name has been spelt in many different ways over the centuries before assuming its current form. Historical records show Sybilla to have been a formidable woman. She had several legal actions brought against her, including one by her furrier. She also had a Philip le Burgeys arrested for an unknown crime and carried off to Camberwell prison where he was kept for the next thirteen weeks in such terrible conditions that all of his fingernails and toenails dropped out!

The original "Heronsdale" may remain as the earthwork, known as The Moat, in Middle Wood at Danesfield. Oral tradition in the village suggests that there was an early chapel at the manor, and this is supported by historical records from the thirteenth century. These show that, after the death of her husband, Sybilla Heringod became infirm and in 1227 obtained leave from the Prior of Lewes to build a private chapel. This was to be served by Richard, Rector of Waldron (1233-83), but was not allowed to have either a baptistry or a suspended bell. In granting the licence in 1233, the prior stipulated that Sybilla still had to attend the parish church at least four times each year.

Ownership of Heronsdale Manor has changed hands many times over the centuries. In 1319 Sir Nicholas de Beche, at one point the constable of the Tower of London, owned the property. Later it was held by the Poynings family until being granted to Sir Anthony Browne in 1538. He was to become the first Viscount Montague. After several more changes of ownership the manor passed in 1630 to Thomas Pelham, in whose family it stayed until 1773.

The present, substantial house is mainly Elizabethan, with some architectural details dating to an earlier period. It has a massive central chimney-stack with a circular staircase following it upwards through to the attic. On the overmantle of the wide, ground-floor hearth is a shield dated 1624 and the fireback, bought from Maresfield Park, bears the emblem of the Marquess of Abergavenny. Although part of the house has been rebuilt, the fine timbered ceilings, walls, and oak floorboards date from the mid-sixteenth century.

In more recent times, the Newnham family, owners of Cross-in-Hand windmill, lived at Heronsdale. From 1854, Caleb and Philadelphia Newnham lived there with their ten children, growing hop wheat and hops on the surrounding farmland. Caleb died in 1903, aged eighty-four years.

Caleb and Philadelphia Newnham at home.

In the *History of Cross-in-Hand Windmill*, C.J. Newnham relates how Caleb's brothers William and Henry emigrated to Australia and Tasmania during the 1830s; some of the earliest settlers in those colonies. The brothers asked Caleb to send them some seed wheat for their farms, so wheat grown at Heronsdale was shipped out and grown in Australia and Tasmania. Further correspondence between the brothers records how Caleb also sent to Australia other plant seeds, a plough, a scarifier, sieves and some wine made by

31

Philadelphia. In 1868 and 1869 Caleb was sending hops to Henry in Tasmania in return for wool.

The Newnham family have a copy of the following story, but we have been unable to locate the original publication:

Talking about the Colonies, let me mention a curious story which a venerable old Sussex farmer told me the other day, about his brother William. Now William when he was a lad, was cutting the corn with a sickle. But he had a nasty accident and cut off a part of his left hand; the fleshy part which runs along from the little finger. So he ran along to the tailor of the village, which was Framfield village, and asked him to sew the piece of flesh on to his hand, which the worthy tailor accordingly did; and all was right again. Now when William grew up to manhood, he went abroad to Australia, and, I think, went in for sheep farming. When he had been out in Queensland some thirty years and prospered considerably, he came back on a visit to England. Of course he came to Sussex to see his relatives. The first person he called on was his brother, the venerable old farmer who told me the story. Well, William came to see his brother, and walked through the farm into the hop garden, where his brother was shimming hops at the time. "Don't you know me?" said William to Caleb. "No, I don't know you, I'm bothered if I do," said Caleb. Accordingly William made known his name and assured Caleb that he was his brother. But Caleb could not exactly take this in, as William had changed so much and got so wonderfully bronzed with Queensland's warm climate. So they came to a standstill. Now it happened that the old lady, the mother of these two gentlemen, was staying with Caleb at the time. Seeing what was going on she came up to them. William claimed to be her son. "Well," said the old lady, "you don't look like William." Then she suddenly bethought herself. "Show me your left hand," she said. William showed her his left hand, and there was the old scar where the village tailor had sewn the flesh on thirty or forty years ago. "Yes," she said, "now I know it's William."

In the 1920s the property was owned and leased out by Mr Freeman. Eva Poulton worked there as a lady's maid, keeping the bedrooms clean and tidy and drawing water from the well to carry upstairs for bathing and washing. Other staff were employed, including French and English governesses for the children.

The house is now owned by John and Dawn Chambers, who farm the surrounding land. John's father purchased the property in the 1930s. He served the village as a councillor and church warden for many years. John's mother, a Waldron girl, was a very talented local artist, often to be seen on a warm summers' day sitting at her easel, dressed in her painters' smock sketching the church or The Star Inn. Her beautiful illustrations adorn the 1953 *Waldron Womens' Institute Scrapbook*, now deposited at the County Record Office in Lewes.

Old Foxhunt Manor

Like many of the oldest buildings of Waldron, Old Foxhunt Manor is of uncertain age and has been the subject of much alteration over the centuries. In early medieval times, when it was known as "The Scrip", it may have been a farm rather than a manorial centre. By 1327 the manor was held by Ralph de Camoys and adjoined the East and West Darn estates, owned by Robertsbridge Abbey. However, the ownership of Foxhunt was in dispute and the abbot brought a legal action against Ralph at Pevensey Castle. The decision went in favour of the abbey, which was awarded the manor by "feoffment". During the feudal period, feoffment, in English law was the usual way of granting a freehold title. After the legal decision, the abbot would have been given a clod of earth or a growing twig as a symbol of the forfeiture of the land. Ralph would have had to utter his intent to deliver title of the property to the abbot, who was then obliged to visit the property and hold court, in order to establish ownership. A charter or deed would then have been drawn up to document the transfer.

In 1485 Old Foxhunt came into the possession of Sir George Brown of Betchworth Castle at Dorking in Surrey. However, because Sir George assisted the Duke of Buckingham in his opposition to King Richard III, he was deprived

Old Foxhunt Manor.

of his property, and the manor was granted to the Duke of Norfolk. It is unlikely that the Duke lived at the manor.

During the early sixteenth century, Foxhunt Manor came into the possession of Thomas Threele, who settled the property on his son Thomas at the time of his marriage to Dorothy Apsley. The Threele family originally came from Wisborough Green. They continued to live at Foxhunt for four generations, until 1594, when the estate was sold to Thomas Pelham for £780.

The Pelham family, whose main residence was at Laughton Place, owned a large amount of land throughout Sussex. Foxhunt Manor remained in the family until 1775 when Frances and Mary, the daughters of the Right Honourable Henry Pelham, sold it to Josiah Smith. William Gilliat and Joseph Rickett were the succeeding owners. The estate was eventually sold by Sir Compton Rickett to Joseph Lucas in 1897, when it comprised over 500 acres. Some additions and alterations were made to the building at this time.

The present house has large open fireplaces and heavily beamed ceilings. The current owners Mike and Angela Crowe have carried out a sympathetic restoration, retaining the many architectural features which chart its history over the centuries.

Foxhunt Manor, The Convent of the Visitation

This large Victorian mansion of red brick was built by Joseph Lucas in 1898 soon after he had purchased Old Foxhunt Manor. His family moved into the new house, with its extensive gardens and grounds, shortly afterwards. It is possible to spot the same architectural style around Waldron, in other buildings constructed by Mr Lucas, including the Lucas Memorial Hall, Tullagmore, Danesfield and Foxhunt Cottages. Tullagmore was built for Joseph's daughter Rachel and her husband Otto Finch when they returned from sheep farming in Australia.

An impressive features of the grounds of the house is the old chancel window and porch from Laughton church, removed during restoration work carried out in 1884, and which Mr Lucas had erected in his garden in 1903.

The house has passed through various owners since Mr Lucas's time. In 1936 it was bought by Xarverian Brothers, who ran it as a boys' boarding school. The classrooms and gym were housed in the old stable block and the boys slept in the main house. The house was vacated for a while during World War Two when, like many other large country houses in Sussex, it was

Foxhunt Manor, built by Joseph Lucas, now the Convent of the Visitation.

commandeered by the army. Soldiers camped in the grounds, as they did all around the village prior to taking part in the D-Day landings and other operations.

In 1959 The Order of the Visitation acquired the property. They are a contemplative order devoting their life to prayer. There are usually around sixteen nuns living in the closed community. Under their ownership, the house has remained largely unchanged, although some of the large chimneys were damaged and removed after the hurricane in 1987. The building retains its original Victorian conservatory and walled garden, although the greenhouses have been demolished. There is now a small cemetery in the grounds and the whole property lies, secluded and tranquil, in beautiful countryside. Very few Waldron residents are even aware of its existence.

Tanners Manor

Tanners Manor is first mentioned in historical records in 1570, when a survey of the rents paid by the then tenants was carried out for the owner, Lord Thomas Buckhurst. Five years later the first Fuller came to live at Tanners. He was John Fuller, who acquired the unexpired lease of the manor and land from Lord Buckhurst. Later he bought the freehold of the property and began to purchase more land to farm in and around Waldron.

Sir Philip Sydney, Elizabethan poet and courtier, later owned the property and when he died in 1585 his will shows that it was valued at £10 3s 0d. The title then passed from his wife, Elizabeth, to the Sackville family.

In 1617 Samuel Fuller purchased the manor and it is he who is credited with the building of the present house. His initials 'SF' can be traced over the door. The Fuller family purchased many estates in Sussex which they farmed before they developed their extensive interest in the iron industry. Tanners, though, remained one of the main family homes.

The house built by Samuel Fuller was 'E' shaped and it is surmised that two of the wings were later pulled down following John Fuller's move to Brightling Park on his marriage to Elizabeth Rose in 1703. Elizabeth's family had made a substantial fortune from their plantations in the West Indies and she and John Fuller were later to become the grandparents of the renowned 'Mad'

Tanners Manor.

Jack Fuller MP, of Rosehill, Brightling.

The house and estate later passed to the Bonnick family who are mentioned in the Waldron parish records as far back as 1565. The Bonnicks continued to own land and property in the parish, latterly at Foxhunt, until World War Two. Tom Gaston recalls:

> It was in Oct 1903 Mr Bonnick died. He was riding a pony when he was dragged from the saddle when the pony shied at a bicycle. The coffin was carried to the church on the shoulders of the workpeople all the way from Foxhunt Green. My father and two of his brothers were among the bearers. It was the Bonnick custom to be taken to church like that and I believe his was the last procession of its kind. . . I only wish now that I had taken more notice of the things he used to tell us of the days gone by.

At Tanners Manor, road closed for repairs, looking towards Horeham Road, c.1913

It must have been a moving occasion to have seen the procession carrying the coffin from Tanners Manor or Foxhunt to Waldron Church with the family, relatives and estate workers in attendance.

Tanners Manor was then variously owned and rented out as a farmhouse until, in 1898, it was purchased by Mr Benden Sharvell Hassell, whose family were already resident in the parish. His mother was Mary Bray of Foxhunt and Netherfield. His uncle, also Benden Sharvell Hassell, after whom he had been named, was a lieutenant in the Royal Navy and had fought with Nelson at the Battle of Trafalgar.

Mr Hassell had been educated by the notable Sussex scholar and historian, Mark Anthony Lower. In 1851 he had emigrated to Australia where he became a successful merchant. With others he founded the Colonial Bank of Australia. He married Fanny Monkton, a descendent of Edward III and they had two sons, Lieutenant Colonel R. de Bray Hassell, who served as a parish councillor from 1904 and who died in 1920 as a result of the Great War, and Reginald Hassell, who gave the village its cricket pavilion and had the cricket pitch laid in memory of his brother.

The family took a keen interest in the village and often hosted pageants and parties in the grounds of the manor. They gave presents, chocolates and oranges for up to 100 children at the village Christmas party.

During alterations made to Tanners at this time, the staircase was built over the open fireplace in the centre of the hall and the property thoroughly renovated. Much of the material from the old building was used to form the rock garden which is such a feature of the property. In 1926 a further wing was added to the house.

It is interesting to note that in 1871 the map accompanying the house sale particulars clearly shows a crossroads at Tanners. The road running from Hanging Birch to Tanners continued straight across, just below the manor house, until it reached Dern Lane by the old blacksmiths forge at Lions Green. The road then continued along what is now the bridle-path to Foxhunt.

Bendon Sharvell Hassell at Tanners Manor, with the Uckfield Voluntary Fire Brigade in the early 1900s.

Cross Farm showing the tithe barn.

Cross Farm

Cross Farm is mentioned in the Domesday Book. The present house was built in 1622 by the Hammond family, who made their fortune from tanning. Part of the house and two of its chimneys were demolished in 1851, and in 1965 the old oast house, which had last been used for drying hops just before the outbreak of World War One, was pulled down. The reclaimed materials were used to build an addition to the south side of the house and two dormer windows were added. The plain wicket gate was replaced by a wrought iron gate hung between two substantial brick pillars.

There have been many tales told of smuggling in the village, and most of these mention the legend of a passage running underground between Cross Farm and the Old Rectory. Tom Gaston recalled:

> My grandmother told us the smugglers used to come up Dern Lane having ridden with their load all the way from the sea. Both men and horses were very tired when they reached the top of the hill at Lyons [sic] Green, and then they would halt and look towards Tanyards Farm

in the valley. If the old farmer knew the Excise man was about he would raise his right arm by way of a signal and the smugglers would whip up their horses and ride off. I've been told many a keg of gin has been hidden under the floor of the granary of the old Burgh Barn, and of a man who brought up a keg of gin from Tanners to Waldron, where he pitched it over the wall of the Old Rectory saying "Now Parson, you can take it the rest of the way yourself!".

During the nineteenth century the Kenward family took up residence. Nelson Kenward had one of the rooms of the house panelled with oak made from a huge piece of bog oak found in a nearby stream, the work being completed by Mr Unstead, the village wheelwright. The present owners are Gay and Peter Biddlecombe.

WALDRON'S COAL TREE.

Nelson Kenward and the bog oak.

The Parish Workhouse

Waldron, like every other parish before the introduction of the Poor Law Act of 1834, was responsible for the care of its own poor and needy. A Poor Rate was levied on the better-off villagers and this was used to pay for the services of a doctor, to subsidise the rent of parishioners who ran into arrears, to pay villagers who took in pauper children and even to provide clothes and wood for cooking and heating. Decisions regarding the administration of the Poor Rate were taken at vestry meetings at which the rector and curate usually presided. Others attending the meetings were the churchwardens, the overseer, who was elected by those parishioners entitled to vote, and the principal landowners of the parish.

In 1678 the state of agriculture was so bad that the Wool Act was passed, providing another means of raising money for the poor. The Act stipulated that the dead should be buried in wool, and that anyone wishing to be buried in linen must pay £5 to the poor. Several inhabitants of Waldron chose to pay the £5 charge. A further means of collecting money was to call before the vestry meeting any man who had made a woman pregnant out of wedlock. He was ordered to pay up to £25 to ensure that the expense of bringing up the child did not fall on the villagers. There are at least three recorded cases in Waldron where men were so fined.

The vestry records of 1784 note that a Mr N. Paine of East Hoathly was paid five guineas per year to attend the sick of Waldron parish. However, it seems that he would not attend cases of smallpox, broken bones or venereal disease, and charged an extra 10s 6d to help women in labour. There are also reports of money given to villagers to buy shoes and hose (stockings) for pauper children they had taken in. These children were usually referred to as "servants", but as their "employers" could not provide them with even basic clothing it is probable that they worked only for their keep. When a person receiving money from the Poor Rate moved away, their parish of origin was still considered responsible for them and funds for their upkeep had to be forwarded to their new place of residence.

The parish also had its own workhouse (Grove Cottages). An entry in the vestry records of 1786 describes the terms of engagement of John Waters, the new workhouse manager. He was obviously an educated man as, apart from taking charge of the workhouse, he was also expected to teach the inmates their letters. In addition, he was to take Sunday school and instruct the village children in the church (there being no village school at this time). The position was not well paid, however, for in order to supplement his income he was allowed to help out as an assistant in the village shop. The parish provided Mr Waters, his wife and three children with a house, and they were to be kept "in sufficient meat, drink, washing and apothecary." Obviously concerned that he might not be kept fully employed by his duties, the records also state that he was expected to make the most of his spare time!

Waldron must have considered that it had more than its fair share of paupers for in 1829 it was decided that £100 would be spent on sending its poorest inhabitants to America. Arrangements were duly made and twenty-eight people were selected. How they fared in their new lives is unfortunately not known.

The 1834 Poor Law Act relieved villagers of some of the responsibility for looking after Waldron's less fortunate inhabitants. Parishes now grouped into Unions which collectively levied rates. Waldron was part of the Uckfield Union at Ridgewood. The Unions worked on the premise that unemployment could be cured by discomfort, and the workhouse inmates were therefore kept in worse conditions than the lowest-paid workers. Families and married inmates were separated on entry into the grim new Union workhouses and the sexes were kept strictly segregated. Local records show that as the Unions began to take responsibility, the parish workhouses were sold off. Waldron workhouse seems to have been sold at auction in around 1846.

Parish poor rate receipt, 1880.

Old Possingworth Manor. Left to right: Mr Rumary, John Daw, Mr Hampton.

Old Possingworth Manor

It seems that the name Possingworth derives from the Anglo-Saxon "Possingwarp" (meaning "the enclosure of Posa's people"), which implies that the manor was already in existence before the Norman Conquest. Although it is not mentioned in the Domesday Book, early deeds dating to around 1150 record that sixty acres of land at Possingworth were given, along with other lands, to the Priory of St Pancras at Lewes, in return for twenty marks of silver. The deeds also record the name of the family living at Possingworth at the time as Malfed or Malfeld. The money received from the priory was used to aid the release of William Mayfeld, a prisoner at Pevensey Castle, who had probably become embroiled in the politics of the civil war prevailing at the time.

The de Possingworth family, who held land throughout Sussex, are mentioned in deeds from the thirteenth century, when John Possingworth granted the estate to William Heringaud (or Harengaud) and his wife Margery.

When Sir William became incurably ill he was granted a licence, as was common at this time, to have Mass read in the oratory (an apartment or building for private worship), then at the manor house.

During the later Middle Ages the manor was assigned to Robertsbridge Abbey, who leased out the property, probably as a farmhouse. The house must have become neglected, for when William Palmer was granted the lease in 1528 at £10 per year he was covenanted to erect a new dwelling house. This was a timber-framed building with a tiled roof. It consisted of a large hall, small parlour, kitchen and two rooms above.

At the time of the dissolution of the monasteries, King Henry VIII granted Possingworth to Sir William Sydney, holder of the offices of Chamberlain and Steward of the Royal Household. Sir William's son Henry succeeded him, but as he was Lord Deputy of Ireland and Lord President of the Welsh Marches, he was often absent from the manor. His son was the famous Sir Philip Sydney, poet, statesman and soldier. A survey was commissioned by Sir Henry Sydney in 1565 detailing the land, its value and usage, the tenants and the rents paid, giving a useful insight into Waldron in Tudor times. It detailed the common

Estate workers at Old Possingworth Manor in 1912.

45

Gamekeepers on Possingworth Estate.
Sam Oliver, Ned Vine and "Nipper" Durrant.

land around the property, which all farmers and tenants could freely use for their cattle, sheep and hogs. The survey also noted that the woods were of considerable value by reason of their use in the iron industry.

In 1585 the manor was sold for £600 to Judith, the widow of Sir John Pelham, whose family owned land throughout Sussex. The original, now replaced, east window in All Saints' church is recorded as having been dedicated to Sir John Pelham.

The house then passed to the Offley family, merchants in the City of London. The first Offley to live at Possingworth was probably Humphrey, whose daughter Elizabeth was baptised at All Saints' church in 1635. Humphrey Offley died in 1643 and was succeeded by his son Thomas, baptised at All Saints' in September 1636. It was probably Humphrey who built the present, beautiful stone-gabled house, as it has early seventeenth-century features, although it bears the inscription "T.O., 1657", above the front porch. Thomas died a young man, leaving a widow, Elizabeth, who survived him by forty-two years. Elizabeth set up a charitable trust which each Christmas levied a rent charge of fifty shillings on the Unicorn Brewhouse in Holborn from the Drapers' Company. After a deduction of four shillings in the pound for land tax, and after any further voluntary contributions had been made, the money was used to buy beef for the poor of the parish. In later years, when inflation had begun to impoverish the trust, bags of coal for the most needy were bought instead. Remarkably, the trust remained in operation until 1999, when the government deemed that the administration of such trusts had become uneconomic. At its close, the capital stood at just over £50, and was donated to the Help the Aged charity. Thomas and Elizabeth's granddaughter married Captain John Fuller of Tanners Manor.

Ownership then passed to the Dalrymple family. It was during their occupation, in 1813, that the remaining commonland on the estate was enclosed and partitioned.

The present house has undergone some alteration since it was first built. In 1830 a serious fire burnt out part of the south wing, and it was not until 1921 that this was properly demolished and rebuilt as a replica of the original. The northern part of the building, however, is original and despite the modern-isation of the chimneys, remains virtually unchanged, retaining its large, stone-canopied fireplaces and wood panelling.

Later owners included Louis Huth, who built Possingworth Mansion; Lord Strathcona, chairman of the Canadian Pacific Railway Company; Sir Robert Craigie, ambassador to Japan and Major Pat Reid, author of the famous, televised book *The Colditz Story*, also made into a film, which detailed his experiences as a prisoner of war in German-occupied Europe during World War Two.

The Bloomsbury Group

In 1919, Alice Kepple, mistress of Queen Victoria's son Edward VII and great grandmother to Camilla Parker Bowles, rented Old Possingworth Manor from Lord Strathcona for her daughter and son-in-law, Violet and Denys Trefusis. Violet was part of the Bloomsbury set, the group of writers, artists and intellectuals of whom Virginia Woolf is probably the best known. Although married to Denys, Violet was also the lover of Vita Sackville-West. Violet had drawn a sketch of herself and Vita in Paris, dressed in male attire, on Old

Possingworth Manor headed notepaper, and this is now to be found in the Beinecke Library at Yale University, USA. It probably dates from 1920.

According to the Evening Standard, "Fruity Metcalf", best man to the Duke of Windsor and Mrs Wallis Simpson, was also a notable tenant of Possingworth. The present owners of the old manor house are Sir Roger and Lady Brenda Neville.

Sketch drawn by Violet Trefusis of herself and Vita Sackville-West in Paris.

Possingworth Mansion, built by Louis Huth.

Possingworth Mansion, Holy Cross Priory

In 1864 Louis Huth purchased the Old Possingworth Manor estate and built a new house on Possingworth Park. He commissioned the architect Sir Matthew Digby Wyatt to design him an ornate, red-brick neo-Gothic edifice, built by the Uckfield firm Alexander Cheale. The result was an enormous mansion containing forty-two bedrooms with a wealth of oak panelling and huge, intricately carved stone fireplaces in lofty reception rooms with beautifully moulded and painted ceilings. Squire Huth and his wife brought to Possingworth the graciousness of the Victorian age, holding elegant dinner parties and lavish dances and balls. After Louis Huth's death in 1905, his nephew Frederick Huth and family moved into the mansion. Frederick was a director of the Bank of England as well as being the senior partner in Frederick Huth and Co., Sheriff of London and president of the Institute of Bankers.

Later, Possingworth Mansion became an elegant hotel which offered fishing, boating and swimming in the lake with tennis, croquet and putting on the beautifully manicured lawns. During World War Two the army comman-deered the lower-ground floor and British and Canadian soldiers camped in the park. It was as a result of a flying bomb exploding on the west lawn that the beautiful Victorian conservatory was destroyed.

After the war, the estate was bought by the Augustinian Order, who used the house as a junior seminary. It then became the property of the present owners, the House of Hospitality Ltd. Now known as Holy Cross Priory, the house is run by the Sisters of Grace and Compassion, a modern order founded for the care of the elderly. It is also used as a novitiate house where postulants stay prior to their initiation. There are on average fifty nuns caring for around forty elderly patients. In the grounds are modern flats used as sheltered housing and for respite care. The main house still retains its Victorian elegance, despite some inevitable modernisation.

Louis Huth of Possingworth

Louis Huth was the son of a London banker who emigrated to England from Germany during the Napoleonic Wars. He was High Sheriff of Sussex in the 1880s, and had also survived a shipwreck when the vessel on which he was a passenger to the West Indies foundered. He had spent some years in Spain and had been a welcome guest at the court of Queen Isabella.

Squire Huth was a generous landlord who treated his many estate workers well. He regularly attended All Saints' church and took a close interest in the village. He gave liberal support to the village school and allowed his grounds to be used for village parties and celebrations.

He was most generous to the church. His gifts included the oak reredos, a pair of magnificent bronze Italian candlesticks (since sold), an altar cloth, choir stalls and a beautiful Elizabethan chalice. He also contributed towards the renovation of the eight bells and the organ.

Squire Huth died of pneumonia on 12th February 1905, aged eighty-three, while he was staying at his town house in Mayfair. He was buried with some pomp and ceremony. One of his obituaries described the proceedings:

> The mortal remains of the beloved Squire were conveyed from London to
> Heathfield by rail, a special train also bringing down the sorrowing
> widow, members of the deceased's firm and personal friends. The body

Louis Huth.

was taken to Possingworth, the magnificent place to which he was deeply attached, and entered upon its last journey shortly after two o'clock, the coffin being drawn from the house to the church on a farm waggon.

His coffin had been laid in an open Sussex waggon and a procession of mourners, including the tradespeople of Waldron and the adjoining parishes together with the estate employees and household servants, walked from Possingworth to All Saints' church, where every seat was taken and a large congregation gathered outside.

The Reverend Humble-Crofts delivered a sermon in praise of the much-loved Squire:

. . . over and beyond these public gifts were those countless acts of private generosity and kindness which will never be recorded here. . . It is given to few men to win the deep and abiding affection of all classes and all ages as he won it. There must be some special gift of God which enables a man in advanced years to win and to hold the love of children.

Louis Huth's funeral procession from Possingworth Mansion en route to All Saints' Church, February 1905.

Daw's Store.

TRADES & OCCUPATIONS

Village Trades

In his letters to the Reverend Humble-Crofts, Mr Hassell of Tanners Manor recalled Waldron village centre as it had been during the eighteenth and nineteenth centuries: "Waldron Street was in those days beautiful and quite a commercial centre. Many of its tradesmen were gentlemen supplying the country round for many miles."

This is supported by the *Kelly's Directory* of 1855, which lists the traders operating in the parish in that year:

Ashdown, Richard: beer retailer
Baker, George: farmer
Barrow, James: shoemaker
Bonnick, Josias: farmer
Burgess, William: shopkeeper
Carey, George: farmer
Chapman, William: shopkeeper
Collins, George: shopkeeper
Dawes, Thomas: blacksmith
Durrant, Jesse: farmer
Durrant, Jesse, Jun.: farmer
Durrant, Trayton: bricklayer
Fielder, James: farmer
Foord, Thomas: farmer
Fuller, James: miller
Gallup, Lucy (Mrs): blacksmith
Gosling, William: farmer & fellmonger
Gower, John: farmer
Hassell, Harry: shopkeeper
Hassell, Thomas: appraiser
Herriott, Thomas: farmer
Hollands, William: farmer
Jarvis, John: carpenter
Jarvis, John Jun.: carpenter
Jarvis, John: farmer
Jarvis, William: carpenter & farmer

Jarvis, William Jun.: carpenter
Jenner, James: farmer
Jenner, John: 'The Star'
Jenner, Richard: farmer
Jenner, Thomas: butcher
Johnson, William: farmer
Kenward, John: farmer
Kenward, William: miller
Mannington, Isaac: farmer
Miles, Richard: farmer
Newnham, Caleb: farmer
Piper, James: shoemaker
Read, George: farmer
Relf, Samuel: farmer
Russell, John: farmer
Russell, Samuel: farmer
Saunders, George: miller
Saunders, Henry: farmer
Saunders, Trayton: postmaster
Smith, John: butcher
Snashall, William: farmer
Unstead, John: wheelwright
Walker, Benjamin: farmer
Walters, William: shopkeeper
Westgate, Peter: farmer

In and around the village within living memory were sweet shops, a post office and general stores, bakers baking their own bread, butchers who slaughtered their own meat, brew houses which used locally grown hops, cobblers making boots and shoes and even a lemonade and ginger beer producer. It is interesting to note that there was a Mrs Gallup working as a blacksmith in the parish! Local farmers delivered home-produced milk and butter. Coopers, wheelwrights, forgers, thatchers, builders and carpenters

The local taxi takes the choir on an outing to the Wembley Exhibition, 1924.
Photograph taken in front of the Rectory (Waldron House).

worked locally and later there was a privately owned bus and taxi service with its own petrol pump. There were tanneries producing leather and even a small glove factory which used the skin and fur from locally caught rabbits, foxes and moles.

Sweet shops were situated at Warren Lane and Back Lane as well as in the village at Beacon View Cottages, now demolished and rebuilt as private houses, and the recently closed village stores. The post office was variously run from village shops as well as the forge, The Star Inn and even from villagers' front rooms. Charlie Humphrey at Mount Pleasant Cottages, Mrs Kathleen Frampton at Forge Cottage and Mrs Hudson at 1 Beacon View Cottages all took their turn.

Waldron would have been receiving mail from at least as early as 1796 when the Lewes postmaster made up a mailbag three times a week for footpost delivery on his way to Mayfield. It is possible that a service existed prior to this; Thomas Turner of East Hoathly mentioned in his diary a postman delivering mail from Lewes to Mayfield earlier in the century. In 1798 the postal route was altered to run through Uckfield to Rotherfield, via East Hoathly. Waldron residents were obliged to pay an additional penny on collection and delivery of the mail. Over the next few years postal rates were standardised and the postal services greatly improved, and the volume of mail increased. The first known reference to a hand-franked impression for Waldron dates to 1839, when a "Waldron Penny Post" stamp was issued to the local postmaster. Any reader who finds "Waldron Penny Post" stamped on an early envelope will therefore be in possession of a rare collectors' item!

Daw's Store

The main general store in the village for many years was "Daw's". The Daw family took over the already thriving business from Owen Ellis in the 1880s. The original shop was situated in the sixteenth-century cottage now called "Hassells". A new frontage and shop area was constructed, now converted into the house known as "The Old House".

Daw's Store sold everything, including groceries, toiletries, hardware, clothes, boots, shoes and haberdashery. The long, tall windows displayed their wares and inside, to the right and to the left, were dark, heavy wooden counters. The left was the grocery department and the right sold clothes and haberdashery. In the centre stood sacks of corn, seeds and vegetables. Behind the grocery counter was a long shelf of large black canisters with gold painted trim

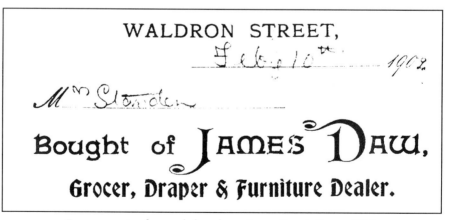

WALDRON STREET,

Feb 10th 1904

Mrs Standen

Bought of JAMES DAW, Grocer, Draper & Furniture Dealer.

From a receipt for goods bought at James Daw's Store, 1904.

Mrs Dillon and Mary Anslow (left) in Daw's Store, 1965.

Colonel Dillon at the Post Office counter, Daw's Store, 1965.

and numbers. These held the dry goods such as tea, rice, sugar, fruit etc., which were weighed out and packed into blue paper packets. Mr Ebenezer Daw could tell you the contents of each canister: "Number 27 seed tapioca, number 26 rice, number 25 coconut. . . " The haberdashery counter was glass-fronted with drawers containing small items such as gloves, scarves, underwear, collars and stockings along with all conceivable kinds of haberdashery. On the shelves were bolts of cloth as well as clothing. Mannequins stood in the shop dressed in the latest fashions. Hanging down from the ceiling was netting which held large balls of string. The string hung down over the counter and was on hand for the staff to tie the parcels.

When the shop closed in the late 1960s the heavy counters had already been removed, the interior had been modernised, only basic groceries were being sold and the post office had moved into what had been the haberdashery department. The last shopkeeper was Colonel Jimmy Dillon.

Bakehouses

Bakehouses could be found all around the village. In the 1953 *Women's Institute Scrapbook*, Bertha Unstead recalled how at the turn of the twentieth century "the Star baked extra gallon loaves if anyone ran out of bread." Ernest Tester, who lived all of his ninety years at Birch Terrace, recalled that the Old Bakehouse in Hanging Birch Lane was also a grocers' shop run by Billy Bates. He remembered how Billy delivered his groceries with his horse and cart. The next owner, Mr Hobden, gradually ran down the grocery side of the business but continued to bake bread, which he delivered by handcart.

There was also a baker at Warren Lane called Mr Tingley who was well-known for his flead cakes. Flead is the pure lard from a pig's intestines and was used to make cakes which, although perhaps rather plain by today's standards, were regarded as a special treat. The fat was removed from the membrane and one quarter was rubbed into a pound of plain flour. Salt was added and it was mixed to a smooth dough with half a pint of cold water. The mixture was rolled out and the rest of the fat was incorporated as for flaky pastry. The pastry was then shaped into small cakes and cooked. Later, Mr Jupp took over the bakery and many people today will still remember him delivering his bread around the village.

Rogers and Son, Butchers, Waldon.

Butchers

In the early 1900s Rogers' had a butcher's shop in the centre of the village. Another butcher's, run by Mr Webb, was to be found at the Old Stables adjoining The Star Inn. A further butchers' shop at No.1 Birch Terrace, Hanging Birch Lane was first owned by Saunders Brothers. Tom Gaston recalls that there was also a slaughterhouse and a butchers which operated from Lions Green. This may have been at the cottage called "The Toll" in Dern Lane, where a stone pig is mounted on a roof overlooking the green lane from Foxhunt.

Brewing

As hops were grown extensively around the parish the brewing of ale (as well as homemade wine) was very much a part of village life. At the rear of Mr Daw's shop there was an old malt mill and the 1851 census lists a Richard Ashdown owning a beer shop in the village. However, the Kenward family were the most

Nelson Kenward's "Store No. 1", set into the rocks on the left of the picture.

well-known in Waldron for their connection with the brewing industry.

Nelson Kenward of Cross Farm was a gentleman farmer and hopgrower who carted his own as well as his neighbours' hops to London for sale. He also had his own "store" where he kept barrels of beer, saved for harvest and Christmas time. The store was situated in a cave cut out of Waldron "rocks" by the roadside just below Cross Farm on the church side of the road. There was a door to the cave marked "N. Kenward - Store No. 1". Ray Pettit recalls the "store" being filled in following an accident when the ground forming the roof collapsed and a cow fell through into the cave.

In 1899 Nelson Kenward decided to retail his beer commercially and began what was to be a very successful business in Heathfield. He was also a well respected parish councillor from 1894 to his death in 1936, as well as a churchwarden for fifty years.

In 1979 Gay Biddlecombe opened the barn at Cross Farm to the public as part of St George's Vineyard. Good quality grapes are now grown on the old hop fields.

Ginger Beer and Lemonade

Perhaps the most unusual business in the Parish was the manufacture of ginger beer and lemonade. In 1848 George Foord built a cottage known as Homestall on a piece of land he had purchased opposite New Pond Farm on New Pond Hill. His wife made ginger beer which she sold to the local farmers during haymaking and harvesting. Their son Thomas took over the business; as well as being a successful farmer he was also the parish surveyor. An entry in the 1882 *Kelly's Directory* for Sussex lists under Waldron, "Foord Thomas, manufacturer of Ginger Beer, Lemonade, Soda, Seltzer, Potash, Ginger Ale and other mineral waters for which he is famous."

The drinks were sold in the village store and both the glass and stone bottles are now local collectors' items. The torpedo-shaped glass 'Hamilton' bottles are still to be found in local gardens today.

Shoemakers

Shoemakers and cobblers operated in the village for many years. William Burgess ran a business at Crossways and Charlie Humphrey, who also ran the post office, had a 'snob shop' at Mount Pleasant Cottages. Between 1795 and 1829, the licensee of The Star Inn, Thomas Jones, is known to have maintained a successful "Shoe Factory". H. Eade also ran a family boot and shoemakers business in the village.

H. EADE,
Practical Family Boot & Shoe Maker
WALDRON STREET.

Boots of every description made to order or supplied ready-made.
REPAIRING.

Advert from the Parish Magazine, 1897.

Mary Durrant of Ardens Farm delivering milk in 1965.

Milk

Mixed, arable and dairy farming have been carried out on the farms around the village. Milk and butter could be purchased direct from the farms and Robin Hunnisett recalls how milk from Farrant's Farm would be delivered to Waldron school for the pupils before World War Two. The children drank the milk through a real wheat straw. Many people will still remember the Durrant family at Ardens Farm delivering their milk. The churns were pushed around the village on an old handcart and milk was ladled out from the churns directly into the customer's jug. Mary Durrant was still a familiar sight delivering the milk in this way up to the late 1960s.

The Collins family at Rafters.

Wheelwrights

Rafters, which has changed its name several times over the years, was originally a wheelwright's workshop. Mr Hassell of Tanners Manor recalled in his letters that "The Wheelwrights was owned and occupied by Mr John Unstead who employed 7 or 8 hands and made superior vehicles."

The next recorded wheelwrights in occupation were the Collins family. Their advertised services read "Builder, Undertaker, Wheelwright and Decorator. Agent for Guardian Assurance Comp." The men were also engaged to make trugs, barrels, hoops, wooden rakes etc.

The present house still retains many of its old features including the oak floorboards and timber and plaster walls. The 1953 *Women's Institute Scrapbook* records that an old indenture of an apprentice to the wheelwright, John Unstead, for a term 1799 to 1806, was discovered when an old fireplace was uncovered. One of the present downstairs rooms is built over the old sawpit and Jack Riches used to relate the story of how, when the sawpit was filled in, they tipped in all the unwanted rubbish, which included an old penny farthing bicycle!

Ernest Cheek at work.

Blacksmiths

There was for many years a forge at Lions Green as well as the one in the centre of the village almost adjacent to The Star Inn. *Kelly's Directory* for 1887 lists the village blacksmiths as Albert Dawes, who also ran the post office, and Edmund Smith at Lions Green.

Ernest Cheek moved to Waldron and took over the forge in 1913. His daughter Kathleen recalls that:

> They hoped that work would come and on the Monday morning the sound of a carthorse was indeed a happy sound. A few days later an ancient resident, in passing, stopped and said "Oh, you will have to summer it and winter it before anyone hereabouts speaks to you". But speak and respect they did.

During World War One the War Department kept Ernest Cheek very busy making hundreds of horseshoes of various sizes. Kathleen also remembers the large letter-box in the wall of the forge which was used as the village post office letter-box and how even after the post office had been relocated, their own mail continued to be left in this box rather than at their own front door:

I often woke as a child to the sound of farm horses being brought early for new shoes to be fitted. Often one was inside being shod and one outside quietly waiting his turn. I remember one donkey. He used to be brought in quite willingly until he got just inside the Forge and then he would throw himself down onto his side and there he would stay until he had four new shoes. There were many chuckles as the Smithy would say "there you are—done", and up got the donkey and trotted out.

Then there were farm waggons to be repaired, new rims for the wheels and often whole wheels to be made. Ernest Cheek also made tools and rakes for haymaking, wrought iron gates, weather vanes and fire baskets. He was responsible for stoking up the Church fires on Sunday to ensure that the radiators were hot on a winter's morning. He was also a Sidesman (deputy churchwarden) for many years.

The forge and Forge Cottages.

HOUSES AND LAND FOR SALE

bordering the Park and enjoying the views illustrated.

Further particulars from the resident Estate Agent, Possingworth Park Estate Office (Phone Heatfield 282).
All houses and sites have electric light, main water and gas. Sites from £100 to £500 per acre. Houses from £1000 to £6000 Specially designed to your personal requirements, but we usually have several ready for immediate occupation, write as below and ask for booklet. P. 137

LIONS GREEN

HORAM   *Telephone Horeham Road 14.*   EAST SUSSEX,

Advert for Lions Green Builders, late 1930s.

Builders

There have been several builders around the village, including Ben Edwards and Son from Rosers Cross, who built the original wall round the rectory garden. However, by far the largest and one of the most respected building firms, was the Lions Green Works Ltd., founded by Messrs Tuppen and Hassell. The company was formed in 1926 and took over the original Rock Hill Farmhouse, owned by Robert Kemp. Lions Green Works at its peak employed 150 skilled carpenters, plumbers, draughtsmen and bricklayers. There were several fully-equiped workshops and a planning and drawing office.

Many houses in Back Lane, Warren Lane and around the village are still advertised approvingly today as "Lions Green" houses.

During World War Two the Lions Green Works made long-range fuel tanks for the De Havilland Mosquito aeroplane and parts for the Auster glider. The latter were towed across the Channel by either a Dakota or Halifax bomber so that they could be released silently to glide and land behind enemy lines in order to avoid the radar. The gliders carried up to two-dozen men and their equipment, as well as jeeps and armoured vehicles.

The Lions Green Works was latterly in the hands of Mr L. Pugh of Waldron House, but eventually the firm was the subject of a takeover and was closed in 1969-70. Many of the men then worked for Marchant and Clarke Ltd, Horam.

Agricultural Work

In writing down his early memories from around the turn of the twentieth century, Tom Gaston has provided a valuable record of a working life on the farm; one that must have been similarly experienced by many of Waldron's young men:

It was in 1896 (age fourteen) that I left school and went to work on the farm at Foxhunt Green. I had 6d a day, 7 o'clock in the morning until 5 o'clock at night and one hour for dinner. The only days off were

Trayton (left) and Horace Gaston at Foxhunt.

Tom Gaston at Cross Farm.

Christmas Day and Good Friday. I remember working the first Boxing Day to have the 6d for myself. For three years there was a rise of 1s a year. There were no Saturday afternoons off at that time, we boys never knew what it was to have a game of cricket or play any other games. In 1898 I learnt to milk the cows which were kept for the farmhouse. There were six cows and it wasn't until then that we were allowed a little milk to take home, before that we never knew what it was to have milk at home. There was churning once a week for the butter for the farm house and the old lady who lived there, Mrs Goldsmith, used to make a lot of home made wine. Gooseberry, rhubarb, grape and parsnip. We had plenty of wine for hay making and harvest and over at the Old Mill, Mayfield they had a cider press. My father took waggon loads of apples over there for cider. I remember one day when he was going to Mayfield with a load of apples he said he would lay up some in the pinnock [hedge] at Stubbs Cross for us boys when we went to school, which he did. We found them alright. There were three of us boys working on the farm. We learned to do all the different work on the farm through the year; wood cutting,

68

hedging, ditching, ploughing, hay making, mowing with a scythe. Horse drawn machines were only just coming in. There was sowing corn by hand from a seed cord, there was harvest, swapping wheat at 14s an acre, mowing oats 3s an acre, cutting peas 5s an acre, beans 12s then there was hop picking. Early in October we used to thrash out some seed corn with a flail in the old Burgh Barn. We also used to thrash the corn with a flail in the barn at Lions Green. That barn wasn't big enough to get a threshing machine inside. Now and then we had to do thatching.

The Chicken Fatting Industry

On 28th June 1894 R. Henry Rew presented his substantial report, *The Poultry Rearing and Fattening Industry for the Heathfield District of Sussex*, on behalf of the Royal Commission on Agriculture and both houses of Parliament. Waldron was one of the parishes which fell within the jurisdiction of the report, and it is clear that the chicken fatting industry was very important to its economy. The whole of the trade lay within an easy journey of the Heathfield and Uckfield railway stations and it was from these that the bulk of the chickens fattened in the district were dispatched. The main market for the chicken industry was Leadenhall, or the Central Market, London. The report recorded that in 1893 the dead poultry sent from Heathfield station alone were valued at £140,000. This represented some 845,000 chickens, weighing 1,533 tons. At its peak, the volume of birds sent to market amounted to 80 tons, or 40,000 birds per week.

A contemporary article in the *Strand Magazine* summed up the nature and scale of the industry in the area:

The first thing that strikes a stranger on entering the district of Heathfield, Sussex, is the number of chickens. In Heathfield itself and around. . . the domestic fowl is ubiquitous. He roams the lanes, and the dusty sides of the high roads are diapered with a pattern of chickens' feet; fields, commons, gardens, and not seldom the cottages themselves are pervaded by him. Coops, knocked up of any possible pieces of wood, stand on any possible patch of green by the way side, and, in the less frequented lanes, in the road way itself.

Operating a Neve Brothers chicken crammer.

The opening of the London, Brighton and South Coast Railway from Polegate to Tunbridge Wells in the 1880s had given easy access to the London market, and local entrepreneurs were quick to seize the opportunity. By the close of the nineteenth century, the Parliamentary Report notes that Nelson Kenward of Cross Farm had become one of the largest chicken rearers in the area. He reared around 8,000 chickens each year on twelve acres of farmland, feeding them on oats grown on the farm, mixed with imported Australian mutton fat and skimmed milk from his own cows. When they reached the age of about four months, the free-range chickens were placed into pens ready for the process of "cramming", or force-feeding. The *Strand Magazine* described this rather unpleasant process in graphic detail:

A higgler collecting his chickens.

At feeding time the fatter wheels his cramming machine among the pens, takes out each bird in turn, fits the feeding tube some eight inches down its throat, and with his foot, pumps the crop full, disengages the tube, and puts the bird back in the pen. The rapidity with which this is done by a good workman is astonishing, the knack of handling the birds is wonderful.

The machines were manufactured locally by Neve Brothers in Station Road, Heathfield.

The process of cramming was carried out for three to four weeks until the bird reached its required weight. It was then killed and immediately plucked and "stubbed". The carcasses were then placed in a "trough", with a heavy weight across the breasts. This gave the birds a square compact shape which allowed them to be packed tightly in the "peds" before being dispatched by carrier to Heathfield railway station for onward transmission to London.

Many cottagers and smaller farmers in the Waldron area would rear chickens until they reached an optimum weight. The cottagers' fowls were usually looked after by the wives, and as the birds were often reared by the roadside they needed constant attention. They frequently needed to be moved to a new patch of ground and sometimes ended up a good way from the cottage. The birds would then be collected by a "higgler" who would take them to a fatter to complete the fatting process. The higgler originally travelled on foot around the villages with a "double-decked" semi-circular cage strapped to his back, in which he carried the fowl. In later years the chickens were collected by small horse-drawn carts.

Once they reached the London markets all chickens fatted in this way were for some reason sold as "Surrey Fowl", even though the breeds were diverse and some had been imported from Ireland.

The growth of the chicken industry also brought secondary employment to the village, as carpenters were required to make coops and pens, and the local farmers, butchers and millers were able to supply the large quantities of milk, lard and ground oats for the feed. Villagers, including women and children, were also employed in the killing, plucking and stubbing of the birds.

The intensive production of chickens appears to have died out between World War One and Two, but most villagers kept fowl for their own domestic needs until the 1950s. Chicken was usually reserved as a Christmas treat. Anyone who has eaten home-reared chicken will know how much better it tastes than today's factory-farmed, supermarket bird.

Tanning

The establishment of commercial tanneries in the parish was an important development in the local economy, and one which made good use of the bark from the oak trees felled when the land was cleared for farming, building houses and for the iron industry. With the numbers of livestock increasing, the tanning of hides to make leather made good use of the natural resources available locally.

The skins were usually immersed in lime to remove all the flesh and hair, and were then "relimed" to open up the pores, even though, strictly speaking, it was illegal to use lime to hasten the actual tanning process. The hides were

The Delves and Head families at the Barrack House.

"delimed" by soaking in dung or vegetable water and washed before being left to tan in the pits, which contained water and oak bark. This part of the process could take up to eighteen months. The hides could then be officially stamped and sold, usually at one of the local market towns. Legislation had been brought in to control the production and sale of leather, with the tanners liable to prosecution if the hides were poorly tanned.

Ernest Tester, born at Birch Terrace, Hanging Birch Lane in 1900, recalled his father helping with tanning at the Hanging Birch tannery in the springtime. By this time, the trade in the small local tanneries was dying out as the larger tanning factories in the towns took over.

At Tanyard Farm, at the foot of Rock Hill, there was another tannery. The Hammond family made their fortune by operating this, and lived at Rock Hill farmhouse before building Cross Farm in 1622. The vault of the Hammonds is in All Saints' church. Even after the family moved to Lewes they continued to be brought back to Waldron for burial.

It was reported that twenty-four tan pits were sited in the field by the river, where at one time a small dwelling called the Barrack House could also be found. Two families who worked for the tanners lived in the house. Tom Gaston's father was born in the Barrack House in 1853. He had always wondered how, with a family of nine, his grandmother managed to bring them up in such a small house. The single-storey building had originally been part of the barracks in Ringmer, which had been dismantled in 1827 and rebuilt at Waldron. Each family had a living room, bedroom and kitchen. Others who lived here were the Delves and Head families.

Carting and Oxen Driving

Tom Gaston's manuscript memoirs provide a vivid insight into the lot of the Victorian carter:

> My father Horace Gaston was born in 1853. My father didn't have much schooling but learnt a little at night school in the village, after he went to work, run by the village schoolmaster. He could write his own name and

Haymaking at Foxhunt.

Oxen on the Possingworth estate.

read a little. He started work in 1864 when he was eleven years old. His wages were 6d a day. He used to drive a team of oxen. There were three pairs, the names of two of the pairs were Rock and Rudy and Pearl and Lively. He used to drive cattle into Lewes Market. That would be when they were sold in the streets. He used to have to walk both ways often coming home wet through. When he became a carter he had a team of four horses. Each horse had bells on its harness. There were three fours and a five, seventeen bells in all. The horses liked their bells.

My father used to get up at 5 o'clock being a carter. He had to get his horses in the stable and give them their breakfast, get back to the old cottage for his breakfast which my mother always had ready at 6 o'clock. He was back in the stable again at 6.30. The horses were out of the stable and ready for work at 7 o'clock. My father never made more than 15s a week all his life and as one may be sure things were pretty tight at times with five growing boys in the family.

Hop Growing

Tom Gaston's remarkable memoirs also record the hop-growing year at Foxhunt. In Waldron it was the women and children who were employed to help with the hops. The money was often used to buy winter clothes and boots for the children.

Work on the hops would begin early in the year with woodcutting. The hop poles would be cut into ten, eleven and twelve foot lengths. Several hundred would be used. Foxhunt would receive many waggon-loads from around East Hoathly for the ten acres to be planted.

In February a four-horse team would plough four furrows in each alleyway between the rows of plants and in March the new growth would be cut back and then covered over with earth.

The hop varieties used were Prolific, Colgates, Grape and Fuggles. The hop poles had to be shaved and sharpened. Willow poles were shaved halfway, beech poles would be stripped or scraped and maple was always used as grown because the bark was warm. To preserve the wood a big long tar tank was heated by fire almost to boiling point and into this were put around 800 poles at a time.

By the end of March hop poling would be in full swing with many women from the village being paid between 12s and 14s per acre to tie the poles. During

Hop-picking at Foxhunt.

Hop-picking at Foxhunt.

April, May and June they would tie the bines as they climbed the poles. This would be finished by the end of June when the haymaking was due to begin. During July and August a mixture of softsoap and quassia was sprayed on the crops to control lice and greenfly, and flour brimstone was used to control mould and burr. A horse would draw a special machine up and down the alleyways early in the mornings to douse the plants while the dew was still on them.

At the end of August entire village families would help with the hop-picking. There were regular pickers who used to pick at Bonnicks, Foxhunt Green, year after year. These included the Reids, Wickens, Delves, Fielders, Ellisons, Briggs, Hunts, Russells, Jarvises, Gastons and others, all old Waldron families. In the evenings during the week there would be music and singing. Payment was by lead tallies which would be changed into money at the end of the season.

The green hops would be put into bags called pokes which would be taken to the oast for drying. There would be two oastings a day, morning and night.

The last hops picked at Foxhunt.

At the hop oast the hops would be put on a 'hair' (sacking) with a furnace underneath. When dried they would be raked out into a chamber and when cool would be pressed into pockets weighing about one and a half to one and three quarter hundredweights each.

The hop drier would be in the oast all week. He got very little sleep, starting early in the mornings and sleeping on a chaff bed in an old dung cart. He would go home Saturday night and have Sunday off.

After hop-picking the families would meet at the oast to have their lead tallies changed into money. At this time there would be beer and bread and cheese provided for everyone. Hop-picking at Foxhunt lasted around a month after which the bines were stripped from the poles which were then stored up for the winter.

Hop growing in Waldron and the Weald went into decline after World War One, when cheaper foreign imports became the choice of the English breweries.

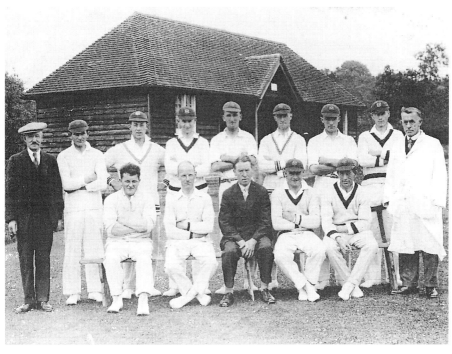

Waldron cricket team, first eleven, 1935
Standing: Ben Edwards, Steve Ades, Jack Burgess, Ron Poulton, Sam Oliver, Bert Smith,
Gilbert Hook, Len Poulton, Ted Jennings.
Seated: Alec Hunnisett, Les Innes, Wilfred Rhodes (President), Eric Pettit, Bert Edwards

SPORT & RECREATION

Sport on the Cattam

Cricket, football and stoolball have all been popular sports in the village, with rugby a relative newcomer. In fact, cricket has been played in Waldron since 1757 according to Thomas Turner's diary. The original recreation ground was on the Cattam Field, situated on the opposite side of the road to the present ground. The origin of the name "Cattam" is not known, but it seems that North Street used to be called Cattam Lane.

It was Mr Joseph Lucas of Foxhunt Manor who, in 1920, offered the present recreation field to the village, along with the Lucas Memorial Hall, which he had built in 1904 in memory of his late wife. Previously, part of this field had been used for growing hops.

In 1921, eleven parishioners delivered a petition to the parish council requesting allotments for growing vegetables. Eventually, a plot of one and a half acres was provided at the south-western end of the Cattam. Twenty-one plots were provided and these were rented out to each villager at 9d per rod.

Around this time, Mr Hassell of Tanners Manor had the cricket ground laid out. He also built the pavilion, in 1923, in memory of his brother Lt. Colonel R. de Bray Hassell, who died in February 1920. Ray Pettit remembers the opening of the pavilion and recalls the large roller which had been acquired to level out the playing area. This was pulled by a horse whose hooves were covered by thick leather shoes. Mr Hassell also planted the present hedge along the roadside edge of the recreation ground. This new hedge was planted two and a half feet inside the original hedgeline so as to increase the width of the road.

Up until World War Two Mr Les Innes was captain of the first eleven cricket team with Jack Newnham captain of the second eleven. Jack Newnham relates the story of Jack Winter who played cricket for many years and was nearing the end of his career as World War Two broke out:

> He was a medium pace bowler who took a long run up to bowl and when he was about six paces from the wicket, stopped, leapt in the air and then carried on to the wicket and bowled. We used to say that this got him a lot of his wickets, as batsmen did not know what to expect next. His nickname was "Magic".

Sadly, four members of the second eleven were killed in the war. They were: Ernest Cole (known as "Colonel"), Basil Oliver, Maurice Allcorn and Frank Lane.

When Ray Pettit returned to Waldron after witnessing the horrors of the war in Europe, including the inhumanity of Belsen concentration camp, his first thoughts were to return to the normality of home and village life. He admits that the first thing he did when he returned to his family in Crossways Cottage

1961 cricket festival.

was to change out of his demob suit and walk down to the Cattam. As he leaned on the gate looking at the overgrown field he was joined by Ansell Kemp. They discussed the state of the cricket pitch. Both men then returned home, only to meet a short while later each carrying a long-handled scythe. Together they scythed the whole of the playing area. Ray continued as groundsman for the rest of his playing career, until the late 1960s, walking many miles behind his trusty Atco mower.

The cricket club celebrated over 200 years of cricket in 1961 with two village teams dressed in the fashion of the 1750s, with the stumps and bats loaned from a museum. Gentlemen in top hats and breeches and ladies in full dresses and bonnets ran sideshows and competitions. There was a fancy dress parade, the Heathfield Silver Band and a stoolball match.

Football continued to be played on the old Cattam Field for several more years before the scrub was cleared from the present site and a new pitch marked out. At this time there were still enough young men in the village to field at least two teams each week for both football and cricket matches. Following

Waldron football team, 1962.
Standing: R. Field, P. Tompsett, G. Stacey, G. Message, N. Bennett, B. Haste, D. Kemp, S. Field, S. Anslow, A. Richardson, M. Brett, C. Pelling, B. Tompsett, M. Field, G. Denman (referee)
Seated: P. Reeves, L. Vine, P. (Bimbo) Crouch, C. Maskell, D. Reed, B. Breeze, H. Carter, J. Pettigrew.

World War Two, changes in agriculture and the general pattern of employment meant that there were fewer young men living in the village. As we enter the new millennium it is increasingly difficult to field a cricket team. Football is no longer played at all.

Stoolball is a game with ancient origins which was played in Waldron well into the 1960s. In his book *Stoolball and How to Play It*, W.W. Grantham K.C. L.C.C., founder of the Stoolball Association for Great Britain, explains that stoolball "appears to have been one of the national games of England one or two centuries before cricket was played" and "as far back as about the middle of

Waldron Stoolball Club (1950s)
Standing: Mrs Fenner, Joyce Davis, Mary Anslow, Evelyn Day, Mrs Best, Miss
Stonor, Lorna Day,
Kneeling: Kathy Smith, Margaret Hook, Stella Davis, Dot Palmer

the fifteenth century one learns from John Myre's *Instructions for Parish Priests* that 'Stoilball' was forbidden to be played in Churchyards." Originally a sport for both sexes, it eventually became basically a ladies' game, with most Sussex and Kent villages able to field a team. During the 1950s and 1960s, the village was able to put up a particularly strong side, members of which included Muriel Pettit, Dot Palmer and Gloria Weston, all strong batswomen, and Daisy Dumbrell who kept wicket. Daisy was well-known for her long white stoolball dress which she used to good effect. If she failed to catch the ball in her hands, she often managed to stop it in the fulsome folds of her skirt! During the later years of the Waldron club, when the popularity of stoolball had begun to wane, mixed teams were reintroduced. Waldron has also provided members for the Sussex county side and Hilda Kemp captained her county for more than a decade. Sussex played on the Hove County Cricket Ground. Her best career

Hilda Kemp in her county stoolball dress, holding the Inter-County Cup, c.1932.

score was 130 not out (as recorded by Grantham.) She was a tremendous force and presence on the stoolball field and could be considered to be the "W.G. Grace" of her era in both village and county games. When men played the women at cricket she would still score the majority of the runs for her side and she was always difficult to dislodge from the crease.

The present Cattam is a well maintained recreational field, attractively dotted with oak trees and surrounded by ancient woodland. The magnificent unchanged views towards the South Downs are well-known and much appreciated by villagers and visitors alike.

A typical Club Day procession led by the Reverend W.J. Humble-Crofts.

Village Celebrations

Both the old and new Cattam have also been well used over the years for fairs, flower shows and celebrations. Old records show that torchlight processions were commonplace in the village. Such a procession commemorated Queen Victoria's jubilee in 1887. For many years until 1937 the Friendly Society club day was held on the first Monday in June. With their banners leading the way, members and their families marched from The Star through the village, accompanied by a local band. Back at the church a service was held, before everyone returned to the Cattam for a dinner, provided by the licensee of The Star. This was usually meat, savoury puddings and vegetables, followed by Christmas pudding and plenty to drink. Then there would be "all the fun of the fair", with steam engines powering the rides. There would be whelk stalls and sideshows and in the evening dancing in the field to music performed by a local band. Tom Gaston recalls the mood of the village on these days:

WALDRON
CORONATION CELEBRATION
OF THEIR MAJESTIES
KING GEORGE V & QUEEN MARY,
Thursday, June 22nd, 1911.

1.30 p.m.	**SERVICES** at All Saints and St. Bartholemew's Churches.
2.30 p.m.	Opening of **POSSINGWORTH PARK**.
2.45 p.m.	**SINGING CONTEST.**
3.0 p.m.	Distribution of **Medals and Mugs**.
	STOOLBALL, SKIPPING, Children's Scrambles for Sweets.
4.0 p.m.	**FIRST TEA.**
5.0 p.m.	**SECOND TEA.**
6.0 p.m.	**SPORTS.**
	The "**CEYLON BAND**," **Tunbridge Wells**, will be in attendance and there will be **DANCING** after the Sports.
9.55 p.m.	SIGNAL ROCKET.
10.) p.m.	Lighting of **BONFIRE** by **Miss JULIA CROSSLEY**
	FIREWORK DISPLAY.

"GOD SAVE THE KING."

Mr. J. M. LINOM, of "Merivale," is kindly presenting Children between the ages of 5 and 14, resident in the Parish, with a CORONATION MEDAL, and Mr. J. DAW, Waldron, Children between 2 and 5 years with a CORONATION MUG.

P.T.O.

Coronation programme, 1911.

Waldron Club Day was one of the great days which we always looked forward to. I can remember the first roundabout which men used to turn round with a winch. Old Mr Bonnick (owner of Foxhunt) always gave us boys 6d to go to the club so with a few pennies our uncles gave us we were quite rich.

In 1903 a bonfire and fireworks were arranged to celebrate the coronation of King Edward VII, and in 1935 the silver jubilee of King George V was celebrated with sports, a tea and a tree planting ceremony carried out by the Women's Institute. In 1937 the coronation of King George VI was once again marked with sports, a tea, tree planting and the erection of the flag-pole.

During this period a May carnival was an annual event, with the crowning of a May Queen, dancing round the maypole, fancy dress competitions and torchlight processions. The following accounts are taken from local papers in the 1930s and show a way of life not seen for a while in the village:

Maypole dancers on May day, c.1930.

Waldron Carnival fancy dress on the Cattam.

"She shall have music wherever she goes": this was the theme of the Waldron Carnival on Saturday evening as music accompanied the Carnival Queen on her lengthy travels round the parish. The melody was provided by the Heathfield Silver Band, the Wadhurst Town Band, the public address and the "hot" jazz of the "Rhythm Racketeers."

After last years' continual downpour even Saturday's biting cold was welcome, and apparently most of the revellers, in their enthusiasm and gaiety, were oblivious of this discomfort.

Throughout the afternoon all those taking part made Waldron their 'Mecca' and at the crowning of the Carnival Queen there was a good "muster" on the recreation ground. Miss Gladys Axell was elected Queen and her Maids of Honour were, Miss Noreen Gledhill, Miss Elsie Brotherton and Miss Marjorie Haffenden.

Mr W.F. Rhodes, president of the Carnival Society, in his address introduced Miss Axell as the very first Carnival Queen of Waldron who had been formally crowned by Mrs H.R. Tuppen.

Waldron stoolball club in fancy dress at their stoolball tournament.

A procession then formed at the Star Inn and about seventy people in fancy costume began their walk round the parish. They walked up Back Lane to Cross-in-Hand via Whitehouse and at the Cross-in-Hand Hotel the judging of the 'open class' took place. No decorated vehicles had been entered but the Queen's carriage was beautifully decorated with multi-coloured dahlias and evergreens. The conveyance carrying the "Rhythm Racketeers" was also decorated in style.

Two of those in fancy costume, representing a Belisha Beacon and a Pedestrian Crossing, helped the others collecting for local charities, by exacting tolls from almost all those drivers who stopped at the "crossing".

As darkness fell the Carnival Queen's carriage was beautifully illuminated and the torches were lighted. The impressive procession then proceeded through an excited Heathfield High Street which was thickly thronged with onlookers. There was a short interval for the various musicians to "get their second wind" before the return journey to Waldron via Cross-in-Hand where the bonfire was lit by Waldron's oldest inhabitant, Tom Driver.

Ray Pettit, then one of the committee, remembers that the bonfire was a huge one with a door on the side, where Tom Driver would walk in, drink in hand, to the centre, light the fire and retreat. "He was a nice old boy", says Ray.

The fair that accompanied the celebrations was a great success and with a lovely turn of phrase the local paper reported "the Queen and her Maids of Honour gracefully bestrode the fabulous creatures that were a feature of the merry-go-rounds." Ray also recalls the firework displays in later carnivals. Preparations would take the whole year and it was a nightly ritual prior to the carnival to make up the torches in Charlie Humphrey's garage below the village shop.

The paper listed the prize-winners one year as:

Children—Girls under 14—
1. Rosalie Pearce (Gnome)
2. Doris Piper (Sweep)
3. Brenda Rigelsford (Fairy)
Children—Boys—
1. A. Stevenson (Scarecrow)
2. A. Oliver (Jockey)
3. W. Gorringe (Soldier)
Members: best costume. Ladies—
1. Mrs G. Axell (Lavender Lady)
2. Miss Saxton (O.K.)
3. Mrs Jenner (Gypsy)
Members: best costume. Men—
1. Mrs [!] G. Russell (Dutchman)
2. Mr H. Haffenden (Red Indian)
3. Mr G. Farley (Chinese)
Most original ladies—
1. Miss Collins (News)
2. Miss Saunders (Tate & Lyle)
3. Miss Rose Barton (Nigger Minstrel)

Villagers celebrating 200 years of cricket in 1961.

Most original men—
1. Miss [!] O. Saunders (Depression over Iceland)
2. Mr R. Burfield (Clerk of the Weather)
3. Mr A. Kemp (Belisha Beacon)

The annual flower show also attracted the whole village. Apart from fruit, vegetables and flowers there were classes for cooking, sewing and knitting. A small steam-driven fair always attended.

Bonfire Night was celebrated regularly up to World War Two. A large bonfire was built, incorporating a recess covered by an old wooden door. Before the fire was lit, one of the villagers would remove the door and from the recess offer a loyal toast to the throne of England.

The Waldron 800 celebrations in 1995 also saw celebrity cricket, sideshows and a marquee housing various stalls as part of the event, staged all over the village.

Lucas Memorial Hall decorated for the Coronation of King George V, 1911.

The Lucas Memorial Hall

The Lucas Memorial Hall and its attached living accommodation, built in 1904, were presented to the parish council by Mr Lucas as a gift to the village in 1920. A caretaker lived at the Hall rent free, and Mr Lucas also provided him with 150 faggots a year for heating. The Hall had been used initially by the village Men's Club, who complained quite openly about the fact that the new deeds allowed anyone to use the hall—even ladies! This caused a great village debate. The Men's Club had been known as the Foxhunt Memorial Hall Club. Subscriptions were 6d per month or 5s for the year. Visitors living more than a mile away paid 1d. The men played cribbage, whist and billiards and tournaments were often arranged with neighbouring villages.

They took the *Daily Telegraph*, *Weekly Graphic* and the *Sussex Express* for use by the members, and a library of books donated by Foxhunt and Possingworth Manors were lent out at a penny a month. However, despite "some handsome volumes by good authors", it was recorded that the library was not well used. The Club often arranged dances and socials as well as parties for the children and the poor of the village. They also rented out the Hall to

1960s party for the older residents of Waldron, with the help of (standing): Mrs Pankhurst, Lil Warnock, Hilda Kemp, Bessie Hicks, Muriel Pettit, Pat Pallister and Mary Anslow. The guests included Mrs Tyson-Heap, Mary Chambers, Mr and Mrs Tom Pennells, Mr Cheek, Mrs Innes, the Reverend Nichols, Fred Piper.

the football, cricket and stoolball clubs for fundraising events. Over the following years the Hall was used even more extensively by the village. The Waldron Women's Institute was formed in 1931 and has always made good use of the Hall for its meetings and markets. There have also been village socials, various clubs, jumble sales, the library, parties, shows and wedding receptions.

Several caretakers have looked after the Hall over the years, including Henry Ades, who had been sexton at All Saints' from 1885 to 1929. During this time he had reportedly dug 875 graves!

At the time of writing, plans to extend and refurbish the Hall have been drawn up, aiming to bring the building up to modern standards and ensuring that it will continue as a valuable asset for the community into the twenty-first century.

Waldron Women's Institute Choir at Lewes, 1937.
(Back row) Mrs Innes, Mrs Tuppen, Mrs Hunnisett, Una Humble-Crofts, Mrs Moore,
Mrs Hook, Miss Unstead, Mrs Pettitt.
(Front row) ?, Miss Rhind, Miss Greville, ?, Mrs Oliver.

The Women's Institute

After its formation in January 1931, the Waldron Women's Institute met at the Lucas Memorial Hall every second Wednesday of the month, providing a social meeting place for women from all walks of life.

At those first meetings tea was served at 1d a cup, along with cakes cooked by the members. It was not all "jam and Jerusalem." Speakers on a range of important topics were invited to the meetings and activities from cooking and needlecraft to singing and acting were introduced, with members taking part in drama and singing festivals and the county handicraft exhibition. The *Women's Institute Scrapbook* of 1953 describes outings to Windsor, London and Southampton to see the *Mauretania:* "There was a picnic on the road side, sightseeing and of course 'time off' (often it must be admitted, spent in Woolworths) and then the journey home enlivened by lusty singing most of the way."

Waldron Women's Institute win first prize at the South of England Show, Ardingly, 1986.
(left to right) Christine Lynch, Joyce Vizard, Jean Paul, Iris Newson, Jane McCulloch and Eileen Adams.

During World War Two the Women's Institute ran a canteen for the soldiers camped in the area and they acquired a canning machine in order to preserve their own fruit and vegetables. They also provided hundreds of knitted garments for the forces with wool purchased after many money-raising events.

The annual Horam flower show provided a forum for Women's Institute members to compete in a local competition. They were just as successful at county level; for three years running they won the top award at the Ardingly Show with a 100 per cent mark!

The members also produced two scrapbooks in 1953 and 1965. The first is a beautifully written and illustrated history of the village and provided much information and inspiration for this book. The second was a diary of the year 1965 with news, events and pictures. This is a valuable source of information about the parish.

Iris Newson joined the Women's Institute in 1946 and is still a member today. Her mother held the office of president six times and Iris has been

Commemorating the Jubilee of King George V and Queen Mary, 1936.

treasurer on and off for nineteen years. Another long-serving member is Jean Paul and both she and Iris have fond memories of all the fun they have had over the years. They tell of the "Miss World" competition they once held, in which members first dressed in bathing costumes, then a national costume and finally evening dress, complete with wigs and make-up. Iris won the competition, which was ad-libbed from start to finish with much laughter. The pianist who had been hired to play the piano admitted that he had been prepared to be bored but in fact he had not had so much fun for a long time!

Many national celebrations have been marked by tree-planting ceremonies carried out by the Women's Institute, including Royal coronations, the end of World War Two and most recently the new millennium.

Towards the end of the twentieth century enthusiasm for the organisation had perhaps begun to fall, but a rallying call has seen new members and a new impetus, and we hope that the Waldron Women's Institute will flourish into the future.

Waldron boys setting off to War, 1914.

WALDRON AT WAR

Even in a seemingly out of the way parish like Waldron, the major wars of history have had a marked effect on the lives of ordinary people: both those who have gone to fight and those who have stayed at home. What follows is the story of the Home Front in Waldron during the two major wars of the twentieth century.

Waldron boys at Cooden Camp.

World War One, 1914-18

War was declared on a sunny August bank holiday Monday in 1914, but very few inhabitants of Waldron were aware of the momentous event until the newspapers arrived in the village the next morning. On hearing the news, many Waldron men immediately volunteered for active service, and long before conscription was introduced most men of military age in the parish were enrolled in the armed forces.

It is sometimes forgotten that there were German air raids on London and elsewhere during the Great War as well as during World War Two. Some parishioners would climb to the top of the church tower from where they could see in the distance the flashes of bombs and guns and hear the noise of the engines of biplanes and Zeppelins returning from their raids on the capital towards the Channel coast. And within living memory, older inhabitants of the village have talked of hearing the big guns during and after the Battle of the Somme in 1916. The continuous background noise was described as sounding rather like a roll of thunder.

Several of the older village men formed a volunteer group called the

Gibraltar Watch, and took turns in acting as lookouts from the top of the Gibraltar Tower in Heathfield Park. Eva Poulton (formerly Jennings), born in 1909 and then a young girl living in the village, remembers that one day an aeroplane crashed in the parish and the men had to guard it until it was recovered by the Royal Flying Corps (the forerunner of the Royal Air Force). This may well have been the Royal Flying Corps biplane piloted by sub-lieutenant Preston Watson, which crashed at the Cross-in-Hand Hotel in the summer of 1915. Preston Watson, a Scot who claimed to have invented and flown aeroplanes at least as early as the Wright brothers in America, did not survive the crash.

At the beginning of the war orders were received for farmers and carriers to hold their horses and vans in readiness for the war effort. Several such horses were provided by the parish. There was also a notice posted up in the marquee at the village flower show in August 1914 from the local nursing detachment asking for money, the loan of single beds, bedding and linen, towels or anything that could be used to help set up a hospital for the wounded. There was also a request for men to assist as stretcher bearers. All offers of help and supplies were coordinated in the village by the rector's daughter, Miss Una Humble-Crofts, and temporary hospitals were set up near the railway stations at Heathfield and Horam.

In her book *The Three Cornered Heart*, Anne Freemantle, who lived at Possingworth at the time, mentions that wounded officers were brought to Possingworth Mansion. According to Anne, Belgian refugees were also housed on the estate and were something of a nuisance as they roamed freely around the gardens, hanging their washing over the bushes and emptying the lake of trout!

As was to be expected, the regulation of life on the Home Front increased greatly. This was a hard time for many of the parishioners left behind. Tom Gaston recalled:

It was in 1914 that the war came, in August, and the most I remember about it was we had to work very hard with very little to eat. I remember one Christmas we couldn't get a piece of meat. I went up to Heathfield and managed to get a pound of dripping. It was then we appreciated the rabbits more than ever we had done.

The parish council continued to meet throughout the course of the war and was now entrusted with extra duties. They appointed a committee to collect contributions to the National Relief Fund, and in July 1915 fourteen villagers were appointed to visit each household in order to register the inhabitants in accordance with the wartime Registration Act.

Other committees were formed to canvas the parish for national service personnel, to give out sugar under the Ministry of Food distribution scheme, and also to organise the fair distribution of coal. There were some difficulties with the latter, as is recorded in the parish council minutes of 1917. The parish council had not been consulted about coal deliveries and, as a result, some parts of the parish received no coal at all. There is also an account of a letter sent to Messrs Lane & Rogers, coal merchants of Horeham Road, informing them that they must not sell their coal outside the parish. The letter also records that "each household was to receive no more than three cwt of coal per delivery." Eva Poulton recalls the rather scruffy-looking van which would arrive in the village and which the children would run after, shouting "the rations have come!"

Many concerts were held in Waldron during the course of the war in order to raise money for the soldiers. Eva remembers that at one of these somebody donated a donkey as a raffle prize. The lucky winner was Miss Humble-Crofts.

The much awaited news of the war's end was received by telegram at the post office. Tom Gaston recalls:

> It was a very wet Autumn 1918 when the war ended and it was a job to get the winter corn sown. I was clearing out water furrows at the back of the old cottage in the lane (this was at Foxhunt) when I heard the church bells ringing in the afternoon and I knew the war was over.

Although Waldron remained untouched by the raids, the parish paid a heavy price for victory. The names of fifty-four men killed during the war are engraved on the war memorial, erected at the heart of the village: a moving reminder of the loss of almost a whole generation of young men.

Unveiling of the War Memorial, 25th July, 1920.

Waldron War Memorial

At a special parish council meeting in February 1919 it was agreed that a war memorial should be erected in memory of all those men who had died in the Great War. On 19th March 1919 the following resolution was passed: "that this meeting resolve that a suitable monument be erected by public subscription to commemorate all those who have fallen in the War from this Parish. That the site be at the Village Green in Waldron Street."

The village green had in fact disappeared from the centre of the village when the road was made up but many older residents would have remembered the green with its fingerpost giving the road direction and mileage.

Una and Maud, the daughters of Rector Humble-Crofts, coordinated the collection and sketches and estimates were gathered.

Ultimately a design was accepted from Messrs Burslam of Tunbridge Wells and on 25th July 1920 there was a dedication ceremony at which Rector Humble-Crofts officiated. Over 2,000 people attended the ceremony and the memorial named fifty-four men from the parish who had given up their lives during the war. A military guard of honour fired a salute in honour of those who had died.

Among those who died were the two sons, Arthur and Cyril, of Rector Humble-Crofts, as well as Bernard Ades (fondly known as Bun) who was killed in action at the age of nineteen. Another was Frank Russell, a family man who went down with the entire crew of HMS *Good Hope* in the South Atlantic just two months after war was declared. His wife was carrying a child at the time and when she was born she was christened Francis Hope Russell. He was awarded the Mons Star.

In 1948 another appeal was made to raise funds in order that those who had died in World War Two might have their names added to the Waldron war memorial. The First World War was meant to be the war that ended all wars and as a consequence there was no room on the memorial for further names. A stone tablet was therefore inscribed with the twenty-one names of those who gave their lives for king and country. The unveiling ceremony by Jack Newnham took place on armistice Sunday in November 1948. The inscription on the memorial reads:

In proud and grateful memory of the men from the Parish of Waldron
who gave their lives for God, King and Country in the Great Wars.
1914-1918
And 1939-1945

Harry Robins - Royal Sussex Regt.
Albert Farley - Royal Sussex Regt.
Thomas Riches - Royal Sussex Regt.
Frank Russell - Royal Navy
John Harmer - RAMC
Owen Jarvis - Royal Sussex Regt.
Thomas Ellis - RASC
James Bishop - Royal Sussex Regt.

Frederick Plummer - Royal Sussex Regt.
Ambrose Driver - Royal Sussex Regt.
Harry Cornwell - Middlesex Regt.
Carey Jarvis - Royal Navy
Cyril Humble-Crofts - Royal Sussex Regt.
Ernest Haffenden - Royal Sussex Regt.
William Peters - Royal Navy
Alfred Seamer - Royal Sussex Regt.

Alfred Hook - Royal West Kent Regt.
Albert Jarvis - Queens Westminster Rifles
Archie Hook - Canadians
Benjamin Edwards - Royal Navy
Charles Jarvis - Royal Sussex Regt.
Bernard Ades - Royal Sussex Regt.
Frank Hearn - Royal Sussex Regt.
Edward Vine - Royal Sussex Regt.

Charlie Smith - Royal Sussex Regt.
George Sogno - Royal Air Force
Percival Turner - Machine Gun Corps
Charles Evenden - Royal Sussex Regt.
Cecil Langdon - Chaplain to the Forces
Leonard Jarvis - Royal Sussex Regt.
Jesse Durrant - Royal Sussex Regt.
Charles Oxlade - Royal Navy Reserve

Angus MacDougall - Labour Corps
Joseph Bennett - Sussex Yeomanry
Alfred Hobden - Middlesex Regt.
Alec Reid - Machine Gun Corps
George Baker - Royal Sussex Regt.
Norman Russell - Royal Field Artillery
Cyril Twynam - Highland Light Infantry
Robert Farnes - RSR

Alec Frederick Reed - Lancashire Fusiliers
Frank Foord - London Regt.
Hubert Akehurst - Queens R.W.Surrey Regt.
Henry Hunt - The Buffs
Maurice Lemon - Middlesex Regt.
Charles Eyles - Royal Sussex Regt.
Edgar Russell - Wiltshire Regt.

Geoffrey Hillier - Gloucester Regt.
Harry Hendley - Royal Engineers
Charles Roberts - West Kent Yeomanry
Arthur Humble-Crofts - Royal Air Force
Kenneth Godbold - Lincolnshire Regt.
Robert Woodhead - Durham Light Infantry
Charles Jeffrey - Canadians

Their name liveth for evermore

1939-1945

Edward Bullock - Royal Navy
Ronald J. Burch - Royal Navy
Leonard W. Carter - E. Surrey Regt.
Peter W.A. Clause - R. Corps of Signals
Ernest F. Cole - Royal Engineers
Oliver Croom-Johnson - RAF
Sydney Dumbrill - R. Sussex Regt.
Geoffrey J. Easton - R. Hampshire Regt.
Vernon A. Edwards - RAF
William W.L. Hudson - Royal Artillery
Mervyn R. Jeffery - Royal Scots.
Bertie Killick - Royal Artillery
Frank H. Lane - Royal Engineers
Aubrey C. Mockford - Kings Royal Rifles
Albert J. Morris - R. Sussex Regt.
Basil Oliver - RAF
William A. Saunders - Home Guard
Garth Starkey - Royal Navy
William Unicume - Home Guard
Reggie Vine - Royal Navy
Sydney E. Woodhouse - RAF

World War Two, 1939-45

As soon as World War Two began in September 1939, men left the village to join up and evacuees arrived from the Tower Bridge School in London. The children were taken in by the villagers and attended the village school. Mrs Westgate (formerly Miss Russell), who was head teacher during the early 1940s, recalls the school at war:

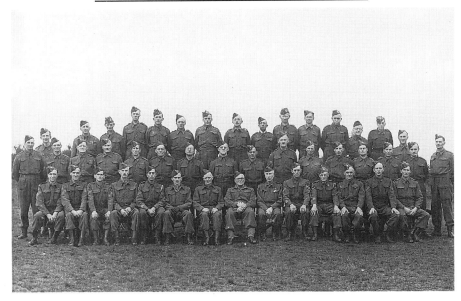

Waldron Home Guard

We hated gas mask drill and working in them, at least once a week, but we enjoyed stirrup pump drill. When doodle bugs came we had to station a child outside to warn when an engine could be heard and the children had to sit around the outer walls, as the only protection we had. The sentry duty outside was a most popular occupation but the hens and guinea fowl cackled long before we humans could hear the horrible noise. The windows were screened to prevent flying glass. Fortunately no doodle bugs fell during school time, but one afternoon, as I was cycling home, via Burnt Oak and New Pond Hill, a doodle bug came over so low that I felt it wise to lie in a ditch. It crashed in the old hop field just behind the houses in Waldron. The school windows were blown out and part of the ceiling fell over the part of the long room we used as the hall and the rest was loosened. As repairs were a lengthy business it was decided to sling wire netting across the beams and the desks were moved under the netting, and we had to work there, rather like chickens?

Waldron soon found itself on the edge of Bomb Alley and the London children were once again evacuated, this time to Wales. During the war over 100 high explosive bombs, twelve flying bombs and three German planes fell in the parish. However, none fell directly on the village centre and there were no casualties. It was sometimes a close-run thing, however, as Guy White, who farmed in Waldron during the war can testify: "I remember several times driving my tractor around the farm at Foxhunt only to have the rear gunner of a passing German plane take a pot shot at me." Cecil Farrant also used to complain that he was shot at on his farm at Burnt Oak.

The Whites bought Foxhunt Green Farm from Mr Bonnick during the war, but were unable to move into the farmhouse as it had been requisitioned by the army as a sergeant's mess. When the troops left on D-Day it was at two o'clock in the morning and they took with them several churns of milk which had been left out for collection. No permission was asked, but Guy recalls being only too pleased they had taken them, as he knew too well the hardships that lay before them. The house had been decorated in camouflage colours and the garden was covered in corned beef tins which had been used as a base to help the lorries out of the mud. The farm and adjoining wood had been used for manoeuvres and Bennets Cottage, where Tom Gaston had lived, had been used for target practice.

Farming was tightly regulated during the war: the government told farmers what they should farm and grow. Farms were inspected frequently and their yields closely monitored. The majority of the farms were mixed, with certain speciality crops grown, such as hemp for use in parachute making.

Due to the shortage of manpower, landgirls and prisoners of war were employed on the farm at Foxhunt. Both Italian and German prisoners were used, with the Germans always being described as very correct and hardworking. The prisoners were taken daily to the local farms by lorry from Horam, where they were housed at The Grange. There were around eighty prisoners at Horam, many of whom had been brought back to England by troopships, following capture in North Africa. The farm also had two landgirls called Madge and Betty. Betty lived at the farm and Madge lodged with Harry Bryant and his wife in the village. Madge was unfortunately killed when a bus on which she was travelling from her home in Eastbourne was bombed by

German raiders.

Also working on the farm were Jesse Brann, Trayton and Tom Gaston, Harry Bryant and later George Paris. Harry, who worked on the farm for twenty-seven years, lived in North Street and later became a familiar sight around the roads of Waldron while working for the council. George Paris later ran the village shop with his wife for twenty-nine years and on retirement became caretaker at the Lucas Memorial Hall. The White family eventually left the farm in 1958 for the West Country taking with them Tom Gaston, who had become a part of the family.

The first flying bomb was shot down in the parish on 17th June 1944. It landed seventy-five yards from the Possingworth Park Hotel. Unfortunately, the hotel was extensively damaged and sixteen people were injured. Curiously, the last flying bomb to fall was also in the grounds of the hotel, which again suffered serious damage, as did twenty nearby houses.

At the outbreak of war all the signposts were removed in case of enemy invasion and large poles were planted in the fields to stop enemy planes landing. Each night throughout the war a warden and one fireman were on duty at The Star, and the parish had its own Home Guard platoon. This consisted of seventy-six men and two officers. At the beginning of the war a few men were armed with shotguns but soon a consignment of 0.300 rifles arrived from America. By the end of the war the force was very well equipped.

Initially, two lookout posts were manned, at Cross Farm and Cross-in-Hand Mill, but later there was just one post at the mill. Training took place every Sunday and this was supplemented by exercises with other local platoons. Some men even attended courses where they were trained by Spanish and Finnish partisans. Hanging Birch Lane resident Iris Newson remembers once hearing a loud crashing in the woods near her home before a file of soldiers burst through the hedge. Without pausing to glance left or right, they crashed their way straight through the hedge opposite and disappeared into the under-growth.

Another familiar sight during the war, according to a former resident, was Jimmy Green pushing his old pram between the village and the camps of the American and Canadian soldiers, "wheeling and dealing"!

Yvonne Herbert (née Whyte) recalls that in 1940, at the age of eight, she was living in Bexhill with her mother, brother and sister. Her father had already been "called up" and was on active service in France when the family were told that they would have to move inland because of the possible threat of invasion. They moved in with her Uncle Stib at the Lucas Memorial Hall. Stib (Steven) Ades had moved in as caretaker, taking over the position from his father Henry Ades on his death. Eighteen months later the family moved into 2 Moatlake Cottages, which they rented from the council.

The large houses outside the village and the surrounding fields and woods were full of troops, either British, Canadian or American. Yvonne admits that she had no real understanding of the reason why they were there. To the children it was very exciting watching the tanks driving through the village and the soldiers passing by, either on foot or on the back of their lorries.

Yvonne recalls being well versed in the American and Canadian national anthems and receiving sweets and gum from the soldiers. The children would watch the dancing at the Lucas Memorial Hall in the evenings, where many of the soldiers proved themselves to be excellent musicians.

There was little indoor plumbing in the village at this time, but as Yvonne and her family had moved into a new council house they enjoyed the luxury of a bathroom and indoor toilet. The family were asked by the service authorities if they would agree to allow the soldiers to have a bath once or twice a week on a rota system, and they of course agreed.

The children enjoyed the comings and goings of the soldiers and did very well from the Canadian and American food parcels. Yvonne remembers being very disappointed when everyone moved out in 1944, not realising that they were bound for the D-Day beaches.

The children were also fascinated by the air traffic and were able to identify the British and German aeroplanes quite easily. There was great excitement when 'dogfights' took place overhead, but they never gave thought to the men in the aeroplanes, as they were too young to fully understand what was happening.

Living in the countryside, Yvonne's family were able to supplement their rations with a great many home-grown vegetables and rabbit was frequently on the menu. Yvonne's mother made large quantities of jam and bottled fruit, as well as salting runner beans. During the last three years of the war Yvonne's

British airman, Squadron Leader A.R.D. MacDonnell, whose Spitfire crashed at Possingworth.

father was in Africa and Italy and on occasions he sent home food parcels containing lemons, oranges, dates and dried bananas. Fruit such as this was so scarce that two of the lemons were given to the Women's Institute as raffle prizes for a fundraising event. Yvonne says that it seems most strange now to realise that people then had not seen any citrus fruit for several years.

The skies above Waldron were always full of aeroplanes as they crossed between the coast and London. Dogfights were witnessed during the Battle of Britain, and the night sky to the north was lit up by the fires caused by the bombing of the capital. The barrage of gunfire could clearly be heard during the Blitz.

A Spitfire P9554 crashed on land at Possingworth Manor during an air raid over Waldron on 15th August 1940, after being intercepted and shot down by a Bf109 German aeroplane. The pilot, Squadron Leader A.R.D. MacDonnell, managed to bail out unhurt in Possingworth Park, where he was taken in by a local resident and given a cup of tea. The pilot's report of the incident reads as follows:

> I was about to set course for base [Kent] and was diving shallowly towards the clouds at 16,000ft; when I saw an a/c [aircraft] directly astern of me in my mirror. Before I had time to take evasive action, the a/c had opened fire from very close range and I was hit in the elevator, cockpit, hood, instrument panel and radiator. I dived into the clouds and broke into the clear at 15,000ft; at about 15 to 20 miles S.W. of Tonbridge. My engine then seized and appeared to be on fire. I opened the hood, undid my harness, opened the side panel, took off my helmet and abandoned the aircraft by parachute at 12,000ft. I landed near Heathfield [Possingworth Park] at 17:50hrs. My aircraft crashed in flames a mile from my position.

Some two months later on 20th October 1940 another aerial battle took place over Waldron. On this occasion a Messerschmitt 109 was shot down and crashed in Court Wood near Heronsdale. The pilot who bailed out and escaped was Feldwebel H.K. Wilhelm, a twenty-five-year-old German. Mr Fred Kemp claimed to be the first person at the scene of the crash:

> I was out walking the dog when I saw a plane coming down and was very close to the field I was in. It crashed into the wood next to the field so I tied the dog to the fence and proceeded to the scene of the crash. Whilst standing looking at the burning wreckage several other people turned up. I was standing talking to someone else and in fact further away from the wreckage than most people when one of the exploding bullets from the heat of the fire whistled past my head and buried itself in the trunk of the tree nearby. This I dug out with a penknife and have kept since as a souvenir.

German airman, Feldwebel H.K. Wilhelm, whose ME109 was shot down at Heronsdale.

Feldwebel Wilhelm was taken to Uckfield Police Station after being detained by Special Sergeant Herring, although the Home Guard apparently felt that they should have been responsible for the apprehension of a prisoner of war!

Army camps were set up at Isenhurst and Possingworth and, on the run up to D-Day camps were set up all around the village, including on land at Tanners Manor and Foxhunt, where men waited to go to the coast.

There were mainly Canadians at Possingworth and as a result of the army activity the village ran a canteen in the Lucas Memorial Hall. This was organised by Mrs Stephenson, the rector's wife, and there was an official allocation of rationed goods like tea, fat, sugar, cigarettes etc. The Red Cross installed an electric cooker so that snacks such as beans and scrambled eggs on toast could be served. The soldiers made it a popular place to go. They also repaid the villagers' hospitality by arranging Christmas parties for the children.

Exercise Tiger: Montgomery & Eisenhower in Waldron!

On 27th May 1942, as the villagers of Waldron awoke to another day of coping with the realities of war, visitors were arriving unnoticed and unannounced in the parish. The army had taken over part of the Possingworth Park Hotel which was now situated within a "defence area", with prospective visitors being requested to report at their local police station before entry. The official directive of the regional commissioner stated "that no person not ordinarily resident in the area, shall enter it for the purpose of a holiday, recreation or pleasure or as a casual wayfarer."

The first visitors to arrive that day were all high-ranking US Army personnel. Among the group were two major generals, Dwight Eisenhower and Mark Clark. Dwight Eisenhower later became president of the USA in 1953.

The following day their British counterparts arrived. Bernard Paget, commander-in-chief of the Home Forces and Lieutenant General Bernard Montgomery, who was later to become Field Marshal Viscount Montgomery, were among the thirteen brigadiers and major generals gathered in Waldron. A copy of the hotel visitors' book reproduced in the 1953 *Waldron Women's Institute Scrapbook* shows the signatures of all those attending the meeting. Would history have taken a different turn if German intelligence had been aware of the potential to destroy the military leadership of the Allied armies as those leaders met under one roof in the rural Sussex countryside at Possingworth?

Dwight Eisenhower had been sent to England from Washington to see why Allied preparations for a cross-Channel assault were not progressing faster. He was invited to view a large exercise taking place throughout Kent and Sussex. The reason given by both the War Office and Bernard Paget for the manoeuvres was to test out the new divisional organisation of the British Army.

However, earlier in 1942 Lieutenant General Bernard Montgomery had decided that the Allied forces must be trained in "a real rough house lasting at least ten days if they were to inflict defeat on highly professional armies such as the Japanese or the Germans." He made plans for an exercise using 100,000 troops and he set twelve corps of British soldiers against a Canadian corp with complete freedom of manoeuvre. The exercise, named "Exercise Tiger", lasted eleven days and involved the Canadian troops stationed in and around the

VISITORS

DATE OF ARRIVAL	FULL NAME	PERMANENT ADDRESS IN FULL
27/05/42	Brig Gen Robert Allochne	U.S. Army
"	R.W. Barker	Col. U.S. Army
"	Dwight Eisenhower	Maj-Gen. U.S.A.
"	M. W. Clark,	Maj. Gen. U.S.A.
28/5/42	[signature]	General
	[signature]	1 Cdn Army
	B. L. Montgomery	Lieut-General
	M.L. Chilton	Brigadier
	S.C. Kirkman	Brigadier
	M.B. Burrows	Major-General
	J.B. L. Shine	Brigadier
	R.H. Lovis	Major-General
	[signature]	Brigadier
29.5.42	E.A. Jukes	R.N.V.R.
	[signature]	C.C.H.Q.
	D. Young. Major.	No. 3 Commando

From the Possingworth Park Hotel visitors book, May 1942.

parish. The troops had basic rations with no mobile canteen, they were forbidden to purchase food or drink from civilian stores and some of the men marched and fought over 250 miles during the course of the exercise. When they returned at the end of eleven days many had no soles on their boots, but lessons in endurance and administration under war conditions had been tested to the limit.

Tragically, the exercise was a dress rehearsal for the top secret and ultimately unsuccessful Dieppe raid of 19th August 1942. During the raid, the Canadian forces, who bore the brunt of the operation, suffered 3,000 casualties. Many familiar Canadian faces were never to return to the Sussex villages which had become their temporary home.

E R

I WISH TO MARK, BY THIS PERSONAL MESSAGE, my appreciation of the service you have rendered to your Country in 1939.

In the early days of the War you opened your door to strangers who were in need of shelter, & offered to share your home with them.

I know that to this unselfish task you have sacrificed much of your own comfort, & that it could not have been achieved without the loyal co-operation of all in your household.

By your sympathy you have earned the gratitude of those to whom you have shown hospitality, & by your readiness to serve you have helped the State in a work of great value.

Elizabeth R

Mrs. F. Piper.

A certificate, typical of those presented to Waldron residents who took in evacuees in 1939, signed by the Queen (the present Queen Mother.)

115

The End of the War

Mrs Westgate recalls what was perhaps the most decisive day of the war:

> I can remember D-day in June 1944: a beautiful summer day. As we were doing sums, one of the mothers came to tell me that it had just been announced that the Allies had landed in France. Before the day was over, the smoke rolled over like fog and we could hear the booming of gunfire.

Throughout the war all church bells were silent. They were only to be rung in the event of an invasion and it was therefore a great relief when once again the bells of All Saints' were heard throughout the lanes and fields of Waldron.

On VE (Victory in Europe) day, Waldron joined in the celebrations. Villagers gathered at the Cattam for a children's sports and tea party. However, before the proceedings began, Mr Burgess struck up a tune on his clarinet and, accompanied by the Women's Institute percussion band, an impromptu procession took place up through the village, round the memorial and back to the Cattam. There was singing and dancing, people came out of their houses to join in, and everyone for the first time in many years gave vent to their feelings. At seven o'clock, the whole village attended a service at All Saints' church.

A Welcome Home Fund was set up after the war for returned service personnel. Every ex-serviceman was presented with an engraved fountain pen and a letter from the parish council.

Waldron and Lord Haw Haw

As Lord Haw Haw broadcast his wartime propaganda from Germany, listened to with a mixture of grim amusement and horror by the British population during the war, there was one person in Waldron who recognised the distinctive upper-class English voice. This was Archie Piper, who had rented Foxhunt Green Farm from Mr Bonnick in the years before the war.

The nightly radio programme always opened with the now infamous words "Germany calling, Germany calling". Lord Haw Haw went on to detail not only German victories, as their armies pushed through Europe, but also graphically described the heavy defeats being inflicted on Britain and her allies.

The oast house at Foxhunt, where William Joyce is believed to have held his fascist meetings before 1939.

When Lord Haw Haw told stories of current British trivia, such as defective traffic lights at a particular road junction or a dance to be held on a particular night, the implication was that he had widespread and detailed information of local events. But of course later records proved this to be incorrect. The broadcasts were intended to demoralise the listener as well as making them feel frightened for their own security.

When Archie Piper first heard the broadcasts he recognised the voice as belonging to William Joyce. Soon, most people around the area were aware of the identity of Lord Haw Haw, long before it became public knowledge after his trial and execution for treachery at the end of the war. Archie had rented Foxhunt Green Farm and, although he farmed the land, he sublet the house to a family called Joyce. Archie remembered that William Joyce had belonged to the British fascist movement and spoke of the meetings the members held in the old oasthouse at Foxhunt. Archie told these stories to the subsequent owners of the farm, the White family, who purchased the property in 1941. Guy White remembers Archie telling the stories of William Joyce who fled to Germany at the beginning of the war, when he believed he would be arrested and interned as a German sympathiser. Indeed Guy remembers the swastikas that adorned the oasthouse walls and the fact that he knew of William Joyce being Lord Haw Haw before his identity became known.

Adding further credence to the story are the recollections of John Burten-shaw of East Hoathly, who as a teenager remembers a group of men who once came to their annual bonfire celebrations before the war. The men had come from Foxhunt dressed in old military uniforms and pulling an old field gun. The men had joined the procession to the bonfire field where to the delight of the crowd they loaded the gun with blanks and fired off several rounds. The villagers later found out that William Joyce was one of them. Other older residents of Waldron still remember being aware during the war of Lord Haw Haw's identity and speak of the interest shown in the area around Foxhunt by the local police.

William Joyce's first wife moved to Fir Grove Road after their separation and their two young daughters attended Cross-in-Hand school.

*C.J. "Jack" Newnham, chairman of
the Parish Council, 1944-73.*

WALDRON PARISH COUNCIL

Compiled from the notes of Jack Newnham

After the formation of Sussex County Council in 1888, arrangements were made for each parish to have a democratically elected council to represent its residents and help make local decisions. On 17th December 1894, the first Waldron parish council was elected. There were nine councillors and Canon Humble-Crofts, although not standing as a councillor, was elected as chairman. He held this position for thirty years until his death in 1924.

At this time Waldron parish covered not only Waldron village but also Horeham Road and most of western Heathfield up to the high street. A great deal of the business focused on Horam and Heathfield as both villages continued to expand, especially after the construction of the "Cuckoo Line" railway from Polegate to Tunbridge Wells.

The expansion of Heathfield was a source of irritation for many years and in 1917 and again in 1959 it was suggested that Waldron and Heathfield amalgamate. This was always vigorously opposed by Waldron. However in June 1973 a joint council was established to preserve the individuality of each parish and to make for easier discussion of common problems and financial needs. Horam became a parish in its own right in 1951.

The first meeting after the elections in 1894 was held in the village school. This cannot have been entirely satisfactory because in 1896 the council purchased a dozen chairs for the councillors to use. The old-fashioned children's chairs and desks were obviously not deemed suitable!

The first task of the new council was to appoint overseers to assess all properties and report to the county council to establish the rates. Another task was to appoint trustees to continue to administer the trust set up by Mrs Elizabeth Offley of Old Possingworth in 1667, which helped the elderly and poor of the parish. Generally ten men and ten women received the money and this was still being paid some 300 years later.

The early parish council minutes which dealt with Waldron village make fascinating reading and provide a wealth of information about the history of the village. The following account has been compiled from the notes made for his own records by Jack Newnham, former parish council chairman. They are used with the kind permission of his family:

1897. A meeting was called to decide how to commemorate the Diamond Jubilee of Queen Victoria. Subscriptions were collected and a free tea was provided at Possingworth Park for all the villagers on 22nd June. It was agreed to levy 1d in the £1 on the rates by the council in order to improve the corner and road at Owlsbury.

1900. Mr Hassell agreed to send two carts and men to assist with making of the road wider from Tanners Manor down to the bridge at the bottom of Furnace Hill. He also put up a new iron fence, which is still there today.

1901. The parish council asked for the rural district council sewage van to be allowed to empty cesspools in the parish. Discussions on a drainage scheme were initiated but because of the expense this was delayed for many years. Queen Victoria died on 22nd January 1901. The parish council decided to organise a bonfire with a firework display in order to celebrate the coronation of King Edward VII. However, owing to the king having appendicitis the celebration was delayed until 1903.

The Star Inn and Daw's Store, c.1900.

1904. An unusual minute stated that "the Parish Council wish to call the attention of the Police Authorities to the case of a little girl who is allowed to wander about in the Parish without sufficient care being taken of her and to take some steps for the protection of the said child." No further reports appear to have been made on this matter.

1905. The parish council protested about the inadequacy of the steamroller being used to make up the roads. The metalling was placed on the roads weeks before the roller arrived, when its weight caused great unevenness in the finish.

1906. A request was made for a speed limit of 12mph to be introduced in the parish. No action was taken and in 1907 a further request was made for a speed limit of 6mph to be imposed. Again no action is evident for in 1909 yet another request was made for a speed limit of 10mph! The council was asked to approve plans to move the lych-gate at the church to the south in order to allow a path to be laid between its base and the rectory wall.

1907. The county council had started to tar the main roads and then spread sand on them. The parish council were not at all impressed with the finished results and passed a resolution stating "that those who paid for the tarring of main roads should also pay for sweeping the same."

1908. The council protested against the haulage of stone by traction engines which were severely damaging the roads. Major Hassell proposed "that this Waldron Parish meeting protest against the use of steam haulage for road materials and request the rural district council to employ only local horse labour in future, thereby saving wear and tear on the roads and giving employment to farmers and their men."

1914-18. The parish council carried on business as usual during World War One, but extra committees were set up to deal with subscriptions for the National Relief Fund, canvassing the village for national service personnel and the distribution of sugar and coal. The council also wrote to the London, Brighton and South Coast Railway asking for more trains to be provided through Waldron and Horeham Road station. At the end of the war, representation for council housing to be supplied within the village was made.

1919. As the sewage van had not been used during the war the council urgently asked the rural district council to make immediate arrangements for the emptying of cesspools in the village! The question of a war memorial dedicated to to all those men killed during the war was discussed.

1921. The main drainage situation was again discussed at length and shelved as being too expensive. A letter was sent to the East Sussex County Council and the Uckfield Rural District Council complaining of the high rates being imposed when only those living in the more urban areas of Horeham Road and Heathfield were benefiting from the money being spent on roads and drainage.

1922. An inquiry suggested that Moat Lane should be closed to heavy motor traffic as it was too narrow and not yet made up.

1923. At a meeting on 28th March it was agreed that Waldron Parish Council co-operate with Heathfield Parish Council in the purchase of a fire engine and equipment. This was to be garaged in Heathfield and manned by volunteers. Uckfield Rural District Council would pay for the fire hydrants in Waldron.

Waldron Street, looking West.

1925. Horeham Road telephone exchange was opened, covering Waldron. At this time Horeham Road changed its name to Horam having invited its villagers to select a new name following confusion with rail freight and misdirection of freight bound for Horsham. Strangely, the telephone exchange maintained the original name with its new spelling of Horam Road.

1926-27. Talks were being held regarding the supply of mains water and electricity to Waldron, but the services did not reach the village for several more years.

1928. A letter was received from Mrs Fitzgerald Finch (the daughter of Mr Joseph Lucas) asking for the return of a writing desk given by her late father for the use of the Lucas Memorial Hall. The parish council pointed out that the desk had been in use in the hall for twenty years and they refused to return it.

1929. Uckfield Rural District Council was asked to build two council houses in or near Waldron village. The Reverend Stephenson, a member of the committee appointed by the council to run the Lucas Memorial Hall and recreation ground, asked for confirmation that they had total authority to decide how the recreation ground could be used and whether gate money may be charged on certain occasions. The committee were given this unconditional authority.

1930. The subpostmaster resigned and a temporary post office in premises adjoining Mr Cheek's (the forge) was allowed. The parish council wrote to the head postmaster indicating that the trouble had arisen when the remuneration of the subpostmaster had been reduced from 30s to 25s per week. The sub-postmaster had been willing to continue had it not been for the attitude adopted towards him by the head postmaster at a recent interview! The council pointed out that there had been a post office in Waldron village for at least fifty-five years (since 1875). The parish council agreed to Mr Hassell's proposal that up to three feet be given from the frontage of the Lucas Memorial Hall to widen the road and do away with the bottleneck in the approach to the village.

1931. Mains water was at last brought to the village and the council houses asked for after the end of the Great War were now built. The Waldron Women's Institute asked if it would be possible to enlarge the village hall. They were told there was nothing in the deed of gift to prevent them altering the structure and they were advised to obtain the services of an architect to prepare plans and secure an estimate for any proposed work to be done. No further reference appears in this respect.

For the first time the question of amalgamation of Heathfield and Waldron into one parish was raised. On 28th February 1933 an inquiry was eventually arranged to hear the objections, proposals and representations of the parishes. The minister of health turned down the proposal and it was assumed that both Hailsham Rural District Council, which covered Heathfield and Uckfield Rural District Council, which covered Waldron, had raised an objection. It was to be over forty years before Waldron and Heathfield became one parish council.

1933. The parish council were still pressing Uckfield District Council to make representation to the electricity company to extend the cable to Waldron village. The company pointed out that the expected revenue from the supply to the village would not warrant the capital expenditure

Charlie Humphrey's shop and post office, c.1910 (to the right of this picture.)

involved at this time.

1934. Over a period of some four months extensive negotiations took place for the extension of Waldron churchyard. Reverend Stephenson was not in favour of providing more land for burials, but it was pointed out that unless he agreed to allow half of an acre of glebe land to be purchased, a compulsory purchase order to oblige him to sell two acres of ground would be commenced. The rector objected on the grounds that the sale would depreciate the value of Waldron rectory and would also reduce the glebe land to less than ten acres. Eventually, the rector conceded, and by way of compromise, offered a piece of land in return for £25 which squared up the churchyard from its former triangular shape.

1936. Nelson Kenward, the chairman of the parish council, died. He had been a member since its formation in 1894 and he had also been a churchwarden for fifty years. Electricity was finally brought to Waldron village.

1937. The Southdown Bus Company was approached to run a service from East Hoathly via Waldron to Heathfield. However, the bus company decided that the service would not be able to pay its way. They asked if the council could give a guarantee against a loss, but this undertaking could not be given. A limited service had run along this route until it was discontinued in 1931. The parish council persisted and with the aid of a petition containing 451 signatures and its insistence that a bus service was essential for relatives to visit graves in the Waldron churchyard, as well as parents to visit the new Catholic boarding school at Foxhunt, the bus company agreed to run a regular bus service from Waldron to Heathfield. Another year was to pass before the service commenced. John Newnham resigned from the parish council after forty-three years in office and his son C.J. (Jack) Newnham took his place. Today we still have a Newnham on the parish council: Jack's son Peter.

1938. Ten years on, Mrs Fitzgerald Finch once again asked for the return of the desk in the Lucas Memorial Hall! The council resolved that the claim could not be entertained. The Working Mens' Club paid £10 to have electricity installed in the Lucas Memorial Hall.

1940. The parish council were asked by Hailsham Rural District Council for all scrap metal to be collected for the war effort. They also asked to be notified of any suitable buildings which could be used for storage of furniture taken from bombed houses in the district. Mrs Oliver allowed the small shop attached to the Star Inn to be used as a first-aid post.

1941. The Lucas Memorial Hall was let for five days per week to the YMCA for use as a canteen for the troops. One day was allowed for the use of the Women's Institute and the other day was allocated to the Home Guard. The contractor operating the cesspool emptying van was reprimanded when it was discovered that he had emptied his sewage on the recreation ground! It was reported that the soldiers on manoeuvres had caused damage to the hall and were asked to pay 10s towards the cost.

1943. The Council wrote to the Canadian forces expressing appreciation for their recent kindness and hospitality towards the children of the parish at the Christmas party.

1944. Mr. C. Ticehurst asked for permission to use the Cattam for events during "Salute the Soldier Week". This the council gladly granted.

Crossways, c.1910.

1945. The end of World War Two. Funds were raised for a victory Christmas party for all the children of the parish. By charging each child 2s 9d a balance of £103 13s 8d. was left after deducting expenses, used for the "Welcome Home for the Troops Fund".

1946. A plan to build four new houses in Waldron village was forwarded to Hailsham Rural District Council. An oak tree was planted in the recreation ground by the Women's Institute to commemorate peace. The annual parish meeting for this year was the final meeting where the election of parish councillors was made by a show of hands. The post office opened at The Star Inn.

1947. The bottom half of the Cattam had become overgrown and the newly formed football club, with the assistance of others in the village, cleared and reseeded an area for use as a football pitch.

1948. The names of all those who died during World War Two were engraved on a new tablet and unveiled at the war memorial on Armistice Sunday in November 1948.

1951. The new parish of Horam was formed.

1959. Proposals were again made to amalgamate the Waldron and Heathfield Parishes but the motion was not carried.

1962. British Rail raised the question of the closure of the railway line between Eridge and Polegate which ran through the Horam and Waldron station. Despite a public enquiry and many efforts to keep the line open, eventually it closed in 1965.

1968. Mrs B. Innes resigned from the parish council due to ill health. She had been co-opted onto the council to fill the place of her sister, Miss Una Humble-Crofts, in 1957. Their father, Canon Humble-Crofts, had served the parish since 1880 and this was the end of an era. The family loved the parish and served it faithfully.

1970. The motion to amalgamate the Waldron and Heathfield parishes was again lost.

1973. After lengthy negotiations Heathfield and Waldron parishes agreed to become one unified joint parish council. The membership of the new council would consist of eleven members from Heathfield and ten members from Waldron.

The final meeting of the Waldron parish council was held on 17th May 1973.

Chairmen of Waldron Parish Council:
Canon W.J. Humble-Crofts 1894-1924
N. Kenward 1924-36
C.H. Swann 1936-41
C.M. Lane 1941-44
C.J. Newnham 1944-73.

Clerks to Waldron Parish Council:
H. Eade 1894-95
G. Oliver 1895-1919
W. Hunnisett 1919-20
H. Burfield 1920-39
C.W. Edwards 1940-45
K. Kitchener 1945-53
C. Turner 1953-64
R.R. Creasey 1964-73

The Gaston Family.

RECOLLECTIONS OF OLD WALDRON

A Wedding and Setting Up Home in the Nineteenth Century
by Tom Gaston

My father, Horace Gaston, married in December 1881 in St Bartholomew's church, Cross-in-Hand. Father and mother walked up to Church together leaving Waldron village at seven o'clock in the morning. My father carried the clergyman's surplice in a handbag for him. After the wedding they had their breakfast at Mount Pleasant which my old Aunt Ann and Uncle Trayton gave them. From there they went to Eastbourne for the day. That was the only holiday they had. They made their home in School View, the right-hand side cottage. I was born there in October 1882.

My grandmother lived in the little end of Pink Cottage. I can remember toddling from one house to the other. Granny had a canary in a cage and there were roses and fuchsias round the front door. I can just remember the first Jubilee in 1887. A procession marching down through the street with torches. It made a great impression on me. I can see them now. I was christened by Canon Humble-Croft [sic] in Waldron church in December 1882, being the second one christened by him, coming to Waldron in July of that year.

Mother was a good manager and never got in debt. She always taught us to pay for everything we had or not to have it. Mother used to make all our shirts and my father's round frocks which he always wore. She used to go out and tie two and half acres of hops every spring and used to go over them all three times which took from the end of April to the first week in June. The pay for this was 14s an acre. She also went out and did a little haymaking and then at the end of August there was the hop picking which lasted for four or five weeks. It varied according to the crop. It was for hop-picking that we had our school holiday. It was all work for us. What was earned in the hop-picking used to buy some material from which mother used to make us up some warm under-clothing for the winter. I often wonder how she used to do it all.

In the old cottage there were big chimney corners. Brand irons were on the hearth and we sat in the chimney corners to warm ourselves on cold winter nights for there was always plenty of wood to be had for the picking up. There were pot hooks in the chimney from which hung a porrage pot over the fire; higher up in the chimney were nails for drying bacon. In one corner there was a brick oven in which mother used to bake enough bread to last a week with a few cakes and pies. It was very hard work kneading the dough and making bread. The bread was as good at the end of the week as it was at the beginning. The flour came from Stream Mill ("Guys"), and the miller used to bring it down from Lions Green on his back, half a hundredweight once a fortnight.

Waldron Street Club Day, c.1900.

Waldron Club Day
(from *The Women's Institute Scrapbook* of 1953)
by Miss Bertha Unstead

The one big day of the year was the Friendly Society club day when the members and their families used to meet; it was held on the first Monday in June at 10 a.m. The members wearing their rosettes and carrying banners met at The Star Inn where they were joined by the band which usually came from Battle. The church bells pealed a welcome and the procession then proceeded through the village and back to the church by 10.45 a.m. when a special service was held, the band taking their part in the music and never was the "Old Onehundredth" sung with more gusto by the men, and any member not present was fined 1s. After the service all proceeded to the Cattam field where a good dinner was provided by the hostess of The Star Inn, a joint of meat, meat pudding, with all the etceteras followed by Christmas pudding and plenty of drinks. There were plenty of amusements on the field, the usual fun of the fair, not forgetting the whelk stall which was well patronised. There was dancing in the evening on a piece of the ground which was roped off and to wind up the day "God save the Queen" (then Victoria) was played and all agreed they had had a jolly good day!

The good old game of marbles—which one rarely sees now—was played, Good Friday being the special day when there were groups of men and boys playing throughout the village and afterwards going to The Star Inn to refresh themselves. Those were good old days, everyone was more contented and happy in making their own enjoyment.

Miss Una Humble-Crofts added a note:

I believe that playing the game of marbles by men on Good Friday was a very old custom and I can remember seeing very old men join the players on this particular day of the year. My father thought it possible or probable the custom was connected with the game of dice played by the Roman soldiers at the foot of the Cross on Calvary.

Upstairs at Possingworth

In her book *The Three Cornered Heart*, Anne Freemantle, daughter of Frederick Huth Jackson, describes her childhood at Possingworth at the beginning of the twentieth century. At this time the Possingworth estate covered much of Waldron parish, amounting to over 2,000 acres with some twenty farms. The park comprised landscaped meadows and woods.

Anne describes the "thickly decorated" rambling mansion and admits that her mother often "retired" to Old Possingworth Manor as she preferred the more plain Elizabethan [sic] house. She recalls that the oak staircase and banisters were wonderful for sliding down and that the long picture gallery was often used for roller-skating. The large ornate Victorian conservatory "smelled of things growing" and was filled with huge camellia and orange trees and a magnificent tree palm. Most of her childhood was spent in the nursery with nursemaids and governesses. She learnt to write by copying the names of Greek gods and was also taught to play the piano. She only saw her father in the evenings when she went down to her mother's boudoir to read stories or play parlour games.

Anne spent much of her free time walking or cycling to visit various families around the village, delivering messages or taking medicines to the sick. She would also ride to the keeper's cottage to collect the game that had been shot or trapped, if the pantry was not already full of the hundreds of pheasants or rabbits bagged after a big shoot. She describes the gardens, where many different types of apple were grown and stored in the apple shed, and the potting sheds, where bundles of carrots and onions were hung. There were nets covering rows of fruits and hothouses where grapes, nectarines and peaches were grown, along with freesias, tuberoses and other delicate, sweet-smelling flowers. Summer days on the estate were great fun, spent riding along Hawkhurst Common or swimming and punting on the lake.

The park was planted with rhododendrons and azaleas, and heavily-scented wild hyacinths were planted round the oak trees. Amongst the sweet-smelling lime trees it was obviously an idyllic place to wander and play. There were also bluebell and bracken-covered woods with heather over the open spaces. Anne's mother catalogued eighteen different types of edible mushrooms to be found around Waldron.

Anne and her brother and sisters were expected to help out on the estate when the men left during World War One. They fed hens, milked cows, hand-reared orphan piglets, made butter and cheese using the heavy brassbound churn and learned to preserve eggs. They also sliced turnips and mangel-wurzels for the animal's winter feed. Their mother learned to use a scythe on the thistles and nettles and mowed lawns and trimmed hedges.

Anne mentions some of the staff employed to look after the family. There were nursery and scullery maids, pantry boys, footmen, chauffeurs, grooms, gardeners and housekeepers. They even had their own carpenter, Winchester, who made furniture, wheelbarrows and carts as well as mending the farm implements.

The family attended All Saints' church, travelling there either on foot across the park or by dogcart, with the horse being tied up in the yard of The

Star Inn. Anne describes the walk through a grove of wellingtonias, then crossing a trefoil-gold meadow, over the bridge at the end of the lake, through purple heather to the keeper's cottage, down a sandy lane and along the asphalt road for the last part of the way.

Anne's mother took a great interest in the village school. She chose the schoolmaster, offered scholarships to Uckfield secondary school and gave prizes for woodwork.

When Anne's father died she recalls how his body lay in a big double bed, the curtains drawn and with three candles lighting the room. Easter lilies were in a vase. Her father's ashes were interred in Waldron churchyard, where snowdrops and violets were scattered over the ground.

My Early Days in Waldron
by Ray Pettit

I was born on 24th October 1916 at Hooks Farm, Horeham Road, which was the home of my grandparents. However my first recollections are those of living at Brook Cottage, Waldron, with my father, Daniel, mother, Alice (née Tester) and my two older brothers, Eric and Cecil.

We had no running water in our house at the Brook and we had to collect our water from the other side of the road, which we were told was a spring, but I think this was really only a soakaway. When my parents asked someone in authority whether it was clean, they were told that it couldn't be that bad as the frogs swam in it quite happily!

Along the back of the house was an old wash house with a copper for heating the water and a table with an enamel bowl for washing. When we wanted a bath we would collect the water in buckets from the other side of the road, wait for it to heat up in the copper and then ladle it into a 'bungalow' bath. When you got out of the bath and put your feet on the cold damp brick floor, it was like an electric shock going up your legs.

We had chickens, a huge forty-stone pig and a large vegetable garden, as well as an orchard growing apples, pears and plums. A peach tree grew up the back of the house but I did not take them as I did not like their furry jackets.

My father worked for Mr Robinson at Whitehouse Farm and then for Captain Leaver at Brailsham House. I went to Waldron School where my first teacher was Miss Hylands, who later married Reg Hunnisett who lived at Tanners, where his father was a gardener. The head teacher was Mrs West who travelled daily from Rottingdean to Waldron on her motorbike. There was no tarmac on the playground and no school dinners. I used to go home each lunchtime by running up and down to the Brook along with my hoop and stick.

On Tuesdays, Charlie Burgess used to pass the school on his way back to Daws with the horse and trap, used for deliveries, and I would hang onto the back for a ride.

We often played pranks but never deliberately harmed anyone or caused damage. It had been snowing hard one winters day and we decided to make a large snowball. We rolled it round the war memorial and down through the village. There was a sweet shop (now demolished) run from Beacon View Cottage by two old spinsters, Miss Jacobs and Miss Burgison.

Ebenezer Daw's delivery cart.

One of the lads opened the door of the shop and we pushed the snowball through the doorway and ran!

By this time we had moved to Dale View in the village and then on to Woodland View, which my mother had built by Lions Green Works. Once a year my mother would take us down to Waldron and Horeham Road station to catch the train to Eastbourne, but then Charlie Humphrey started the Eagle bus service from Waldron to Eastbourne. He had a Chevrolet with blue fabric and then a coach called Bluebell together with a charabanc. They were all parked below the village shop in a shed where there was a petrol pump.

A yearly flower show was held on the Cattam field opposite the village hall where football was still being played. There were two tents for exhibits, mostly flowers and vegetables, and the children picked wild flowers to show. Jones' Fair set up rides and sideshows and there were swings, roundabouts, coconut shies etc. There were traction engines and a large engine to work the dynamo for all the lights. Clinker was thrown on the ground to help the machines up the slight incline into the Cattam gate.

I remember my father exhibiting, along with Walter Day, the head gardener from Foxhunt, Jack Russell from Firgrove Road and Fred Piper from Grove Cottage.

The Tester family were 'chapel goers' and I remember my grandfather Tester packing his sandwiches into his Gladstone bag before spending all day Sunday at Little London chapel. We also used to walk to the chapel at Blackboys and the chapel along the Blackboys to Halland road.

Lord Strathcona lived at Possingworth and I can remember him bringing rocks all the way up from the West Country in order to make the rockery. The head keeper was 'Bomber' Wells and I went to school with his son Cyril. We helped out with the pheasant shoots and beating for the pigeon shoots held at Blackboys on Good Friday. It was here that I learned to pigeon shoot. Birds were raised for the shoot and then set free across the fields. A large circle was marked out and the idea was to see how many pigeons could be shot down within the circle. The dead pigeons were then cooked in a large boiler and fed, along with peas, maize and wheat, to the pheasants.

I remember lying for hours on my stomach by a stream holding a stick with a wire noose trying to catch a trout. It took a good deal of patience and a steady hand but I caught several trout that way. I do not recall anybody else catching one.

I also used to go to Ardens Farm and run behind Mr Durrant's machine as he cut the corn hoping for a rabbit to run out. I would 'dab' it on the head with a stick and take it home for dinner.

Ray, in his younger days, was a crack shot and anybody who saw him shoot pigeon, even in high winds, would testify to a hit rate of at least 95 per cent. He was, as a consequence, in high demand with the local farmers, assisting them in reducing foxes and keeping the pigeons from the crops. He was a real countryman and his passing will see the end of a generation who could talk to the animals.

The Waldron Fire Brigade
by Jack Newnham

In 1938, as one of the preparations in case of war, the Auxiliary Fire Service was formed. We had about a dozen members at Cross-in-Hand and the same number in Waldron. The members of the Heathfield Brigade gave us some training, and the Hailsham District Council, who at this time were in control, sent to both Waldron and Cross-in-Hand a manual fire pump with handles each side, about four lengths of hose, a canvas water container and a dozen canvas buckets. Both Waldron and Cross-in-Hand built a trailer to put the equipment in, so that it could be towed by a car. When the war started in 1939 we had a fireman on duty each night in our mill. He had a bed beside the telephone so that he could contact the other firemen if necessary, or the wardens post or the Home Guard.

I can remember that after the Canadian forces had come to the camp in Possingworth, we had held a practice and the canvas buckets were wet, so I had them put outside of the building to dry. When I went to put them away, they were missing, so I went to the camp at Possingworth and an officer found them for me. No doubt the troops thought they were just the thing for washing in.

A short time after the war started, the National Fire Service was formed, they took over the fire station at Heathfield. Another building was put up on the other side of the road at Tilsmore Corner and the station was now manned by full-time firemen, the old Heathfield Brigade firemen taking over some night duties under the full-time officer in charge.

At this time large exercises were held at Brighton, Eastbourne and Hastings, and as the Cross-in-Hand and Waldron firemen trained at Heathfield with the modern trailer pumps, we were asked to send a crew to a large exercise in Brighton. Mostly we had towed the trailer pump with a large Humber car,

Reg Hunisett in his Auxilliary Fire Service
Uniform, June 1940.

but this had gone to Eastbourne for servicing. They had sent a dilapidated thirty cwt. Ford lorry to take its place. When we left the fire station at Heathfield with Dick Pearson driving, the handbrake lever came off in his hand as he took the brake off. We had all been keen to go, so said nothing about it. We had to go to a meeting place at The Drive, Hove, which was a wide straight road. When we got there, there must have been about 200 highly polished fire engines, whose crews were dressed in smart firemen's uniforms. We, on the other hand, had no uniforms, only boiler suits, wellington boots, tin hats, a fireman's belt and axe, and a dilapidated lorry without a handbrake. As we drew up, Dick shouted to Bill Andrews who was riding in the back of the lorry, "Bill, put the ramps under the back wheels!". The ramps were used to cover the hoses when they cross a road. As Bill did this, the well-dressed firemen stared in amazement and exclaimed "Whatever have we got here?". To this Dick replied "Its not the uniform that makes the fireman mates!"

We were then sent to a supposed incident at Portslade and told that when we had finished to report back at the fire brigade headquarters at Roedean, (now the Girl's College), for a meal before returning home. When we had finished our meal and were ready to go, we could not find Bill Andrews, who was last seen following some firewomen upstairs. It was by now 2 a.m., and being fed up looking for him, we decided to leave him and go home. When we got back to the lorry, much to our surprise, he was there waiting for us.

About a week after this, there was another exercise to be held at East-bourne, I was asked by the station officer to get a crew together and go. I went on a bicycle to Waldron and got a crew, but on the day of the exercise the station officer telephoned me, and said that the divisional officer had notified him, that as we had no uniforms we could not go. This made me angry as I had to cycle round again to stop the crew reporting at Heathfield. Our appearance at Brighton had probably got to his notice. I told the station officer to tell the divisional officer that if we were not fit to be seen in Brighton, Eastbourne and Hastings, neither were we fit to be seen in Heathfield, Cross-in-Hand or Waldron and until we were fitted out with proper uniforms we should not do any more drills etc. The lads serving in the Punnetts Town Brigade who were in a similar position to us agreed to do the same. This in a few days produced results, for I had enough uniforms of all sizes sent to me to fit out several Brigades.

The 1950s & 60s
by Brian Tompsett

It was in May 1954, aged six years, that I moved to Tanyard Farm at Waldron with my parents, three brothers and two sisters. We moved from a fairly modern house to one without electricity, mains water or drainage. This obviously made life more difficult for my mother having five children of school age.

The farm was owned by a Mr Jones who lived at Hazelbrook, Back Lane, Cross-in-Hand. It consisted of about fifty acres for dairy, beef and poultry production. Although the farm had a little Allis Chalmers tractor, most of the work was still being done with the good old faithful cart horse.

The village school consisted of two classes with Mrs Gifford, the head mistress, teaching the top class and Miss Truby the infants. Everyone walked to school as most lived within a mile. The only car parked outside was the baby Austin A30 used by Mrs Gifford, who travelled from Lewes. Miss Truby cycled from Framfield. The cook was Mrs Leeves from Moat Lane who was assisted by the secretary Mrs Higgins from Foxhunt. The caretaker, Mrs Langridge, lived in the adjoining school house.

Life at the school was generally a happy and contented one. The school dinners were out of this world and any leftovers were soon snapped up for 'seconds'. During the winter months our morning milk was supplied hot from the kitchen and we were allowed to take a mixture of cocoa and sugar to add to it. Religion was an important part of school life and regularly the whole school walked in pairs around the wall to attend a service at the church conducted by the rector, the Reverend Percy Willmott Jenkins. He resided in the vicarage situated on the Cross-in-Hand road at Heathfield.

Music, singing and dancing was another regular subject which was sometimes performed at the Lucas Hall. The older children annually took part in a music festival at Heathfield Secondary Modern School. I can remember a Miss Webster from New Zealand coming to teach us, probably on some kind of exchange visit. She taught us a Maori song which we eventually had to perform in public. We had to kneel in pairs facing each other with a baton in each hand. Initially these were rolled up newspaper and taped to form something suitable to practise with. While singing, the batons were used in sequence, being tapped together and on the floor and then exchanged with your partner by passing and catching. Once you got into the spirit of it, the sound of wood on wood became quite loud. When performed in public the inevitable red faces appeared when some of the batons were dropped. It was certainly something a little different and good fun. After all this time I can still remember some of the words!

The playing of games and sport was very limited due to the size of the playground and the Lucas Hall. On fine sunny days we were able to use the Cattam and rounders was a regular team game. I was really pleased with myself one day when I hit the ball so hard out of bounds that it was never found. My main dislike at school was performing to the public, whether it be the Christmas nativity play or for the village church fête. One year I had to dance in the grounds of Crossways, the home of the Humble-Crofts, where the fête was then held. I always did my best to try and get out of it but obviously I failed on that occasion.

The school always had an annual coach outing to such places as Windsor Castle, the Tower of London or London Zoo. The annoying thing, though, was having to write all about it the following day.

Discipline at school was fairly strict and resulted in me getting the cane on at least two occasions (I am sure it was only two). Generally speaking most children that left Waldron for the 'big' school at Heathfield did well in spite of the limited size and resources.

Village life was somewhat different to today. The post office was in The Star public house and only one or the other could be open, but not both. It later moved next door and was run by Mrs Frampton. She was the daughter of Mr Cheek, the village blacksmith, who lived at the forge adjoining. The Daw family ran the main shop situated near the memorial where you could buy just about anything. Mrs Paris ran the sweet shop situated in what was the last remaining shop in Waldron (alas it has just closed—July 1999). She also sold cigarettes and paraffin from an old fuel pump and later she moved to the Lucas Hall as caretaker.

Fred Piper was the local roadman living at Victor Cottage. Road users were warned of his presence by two red flags as he cut the verges and cleared the ditches by hand. The postmen were Tom Latter and Billy Andrews who delivered the mail by pushbike from Cross-in-Hand.

Mr Jupp was the baker, delivering from his premises in Warren Lane. Milk

Mrs Gwen Paris outside the village shop.

George Paris at the village petrol pump.

was delivered in the centre of the village by the Durrants from Ardens Farm. They used a three-wheeled handcart and the milk was ladled straight from the churn.

There was a three-hourly bus service four times a day. The number 95 bus returned to Eastbourne via Heathfield, Rushlake Green, Hailsham and Stone Cross. There were five buses on Saturday with the last one leaving at 10.30 p.m., sometimes being a double-decker.

At play we could roam anywhere around the garden, farm, road, woods, stream and even the lake at Tanners Manor without any fear of coming to any harm. Being part of a large family we used to get up to all sorts of things. I could make a dart out of hazel and carefully split the end to hold a cardboard flight. Using a knotted piece of string like a sling I could propel the dart through the air a great distance. We used to make blowpipes from wild parsley stalks and use hawthorn berries for ammunition.

Some summer evenings we used to get a lot of coaches travelling through on mystery tours. From a vantage point we used to wave to the passengers with the intention of getting as many as possible waving back at us. All good harmless fun.

On the farm I enjoyed helping my dad especially if he was using the cart horse. As I grew older I used to help my dad 'thistle dodging'. Armed with a swap [sickle] and he with a scythe we used to cover all of the grass fields cutting the thistles, nettles and docks. To reward me for my work I can well remember Mr Jones giving me my first ever pound note, a lot of money in those days.

Life on the farm and at home improved somewhat when a diesel-powered generator was installed. This meant that we no longer had to take the accumulator (a glass, acid-filled type of battery) to Burt's cycle shop in Horam for recharging so we could listen to the wireless. We could also get a television. This modern generator was such that when the last light was turned off at night, it would automatically stop. Well, that was the theory but often dad had to dress again and traipse down to the farm to restore peace and tranquility to the countryside once more.

Mr Jones collapsed and died on the farm one Saturday afternoon, during the summer of 1958. The farm was then sold and we moved to Foxhunt Cottage where dad worked for Mr Chambers of Heronsdale Manor. The Dewe family bought Tanyard Farm and over forty years later are still there.

Other children of my age group that I went to school with were Barry Hembling, Geoff Holt, Rex Edwards, Sheila Tapp and Pamela Rees.

There are now only a handful of people living in the village that that were there all those years ago. These are Mrs Hughes and Mr Spink of Brittenden Lane, Mrs Weston and Doreen Freshwater of North Street and Iris Newson of Hanging Birch Lane. In addition there are the farming families of Burgess, Delves, Dewe, Chambers and Farrant.

My parents eventually left Waldron in 1970, by which time I had already started my career in the police service. This was highlighted with my last ten years serving as the last 'village bobby' to cover the village in which I grew up. I lived in the police house at Cross-in-Hand, once occupied by Bert Hutchins for many years. This house I now own so I am able to maintain my ties with Waldron. Sadly life in the village as I knew it all those years ago will never be the same.

The 1950s & 60s - some additional thoughts
by Susan Russell

I remember Waldron when we had Mr Paris's sweetshop, and Daw's Store provided and delivered all our grocery and haberdashery needs. Mr Jupp brought round fresh bread from his bakery at Rosers Cross and the Durrant family in North Street delivered milk straight from their farm. Meat was delivered to the back door and dad (Ray Pettit) grew all our vegetables at home and on his allotment at the bottom of the Cattam. We seemed so self-sufficient!

In Harry Bryant's front room, my Dad could have a haircut, hot sausage roll and a glass of wine—all for 6d. The village had a district nurse, a village policeman on his bicycle, three buses a day, a rector living in the old rectory and Mr Cheek working the forge. We had the village school and I remember outings to the seaside, parties and Christmas plays for the whole village. There was a cricket and ladies stoolball team, as well as two football teams (never rugby).

The Lucas Memorial Hall was used for whist drives, the library, jumble sales, Women's Institute and concerts. We had Saturday night socials, dancing the valeta and gay gordons to piano, mandolin and drums, playing silly games, drinking tea and eating egg sandwiches in the interval; and all for 9d.

I was never bored as a child and I am sure the sun shone every day!

THE LAST TWENTY YEARS

One of Waldron's fingerposts.
There are said to be 183 signs to the village.

The Star Inn, Waldron 800 celebrations, 1995.

THE PUB AND THE VILLAGE COMMUNITY

Samuel Johnson was obviously a man who enjoyed his pub. "A tavern chair is the throne of human felicity" he wrote once, and "There is nothing which has yet been contrived by man by which so much happiness is produced as by a good tavern or inn."

Nothing changes. While many village schools were closed during the second half of the twentieth century, and, in the last decade, too many village shops went down in the face of heavy competition from the easy shopping in supermarkets, nevertheless a village can still claim to be a village if it has a well-run pub, and Waldron's Star Inn is certainly that. Standing at the crossroads in the centre of the village it welcomes the lonely, consoles the sad, amuses all ages, celebrates when there's something to shout about, and feeds the hungry. It is one of the few places, even today, where the solitary female can feel entirely at home and is made welcome.

It operates as a watering hole, an entertainment centre, a gossip shop and a place to exchange information. If you need a good plumber, a reliable carpenter, someone to house-sit while you're away on holiday or someone to print a logo on your T-shirt, ask Paul behind the bar.

If you want somewhere to meet up before you go on somewhere else, The Star is warm and welcoming. If you come early for a wedding at the church, you can change and have a jar before arriving dead on time as the bells ring out. If you're late and you don't want to disturb the service, The Star is a haven out of the rain where you can watch for the first guests to emerge from the lych-gate and be there with your camera as the bride walks down the path.

The Star on New Year's Eve is packed with cheerful revellers, some clad in the weirdest of costumes. On the stroke of midnight as the church clock strikes twelve, the entire pub empties of people as they gather in the square to sing 'Auld Lang Syne' and wish each other a happy new year. It was the venue for many to see in the new century and to watch and cheer the fireworks hurtling and exploding in the sky from gardens around the village centre.

On a summer's day, it rings with children's voices as they play in the orchard behind, while their parents chat under the apple trees over a sandwich or a pie. The field has been used for parties and barbecues and, for the first time ever in 1999, even an open-air performance of a Shakespeare play, when the Rude Mechanicals theatre company put on *A Comedy of Errors* on a balmy August evening.

At the start of the new century it is the last business open to the public left in the village, and like so many village businesses, it is run by a family. Con and Paul Lefort (father and son) are the licensees, with Lesley as queen of the kitchen and The Star's famous summer barbecues, her mum Ann bringing out the trays of food, Con's wife Iris still putting in an occasional appearance behind the bar and the third generation of Amie, William and George also in evidence. (Amie is a promising darts player whenever there's a chance and George loves to play in on his drums with the jazz band.)

In 1995 at the time of Waldron 800 The Star hosted open-air jazz and a barn dance, and welcomed the world and his wife who came to join in the village celebration. In July 2000 it will again be playing a key role in the Waldron Millennium Festival, welcoming the school reunion, hosting a folk night open to everyone, and being the venue for the end of festival picnic party.

The launch of the Waldron 800 wine. (Left to right: Diana Elmitt, Alexandra Yuill, Anne Ellis, Gay Biddlecombe, James Yuill.)

THE RISE OF ST GEORGE'S VINEYARD

For centuries, the villagers of Waldron were employed directly in the agricultural industry or one closely connected to it. Look back to the 1851 census for the village and you find occupations including farmer, groom, oxman (and under-oxman,) wheelwright, farm bailiff, smith, wood reeve, miller, farm servant, agricultural bailiff and any number of agricultural labourers amongst the residents. But nowhere is there mention of a viniculturist, for it was not until the second half of the twentieth century that Waldron had its own vineyard.

149

Gay Biddlecombe and her husband Peter were both journalists living and working in London in the mid-1970s when they tasted English wine for the first time. That first taste changed their lives, for Gay became convinced of the enormous potential not only for the production of wine in England, but also for its marketing. Once she had made up her mind to establish an experimental vineyard, she brought formidable determination, drive and marketing knowledge to bear on the business of viniculture.

In 1979 the Biddlecombes bought Cross Farm, an estate with a barn which is mentioned in the Domesday Book. The initial five-acre planting was so successful that the vineyard was extended to twenty acres in 1985, making it one of the largest in Sussex. The first harvest was in 1982 and over the subsequent sixteen years, St George's English Wines became established and a familiar name on the dinner tables of the nation and abroad.

It was a brilliant marketing decision to put the patron saint of England and the English flag on the label, and Gay's promotional expertise soon opened doors for her wine, including the House of Commons, Mr Speaker's House, No. 10 Downing Street, and the Tower of London, as well as top hotels including the Trusthouse Forte chain. Exports took the wine and the name of the small village of Waldron to Australia, New Zealand, Canada, the USA, Malaya, West Africa, Germany, Italy, Holland and Japan.

In 1986 a unique wine club was established called "Adopt-a-vine" which offered the man or woman who had everything the opportunity of having a vine named after them and receiving a bottle of wine with their own personalised label. Some 25,000 members enrolled over the years, and the vineyard also welcomed more than 35,000 visitors a year from 1984 when Gay opened the gates to the public. The publication of Gay's book, *A Vine Romance—Tales from an English Vineyard* created a further audience and took the fame of St George's Vineyard and Waldron to most English-speaking countries, as well as Germany and Sweden.

In 1999 Gay Biddlecombe decided that twenty years was enough of her life to dedicate to wine production and the gates were closed to visitors. But it wasn't the end of the romance: the vines were leased to Plumpton Agricultural College for its viticulture course, in the establishment of which Gay had had a hand. Today the vines go on, and grapes from Waldron are to be used in Plumpton's own wines.

Crossways. Moat Lane blocked.

THE GREAT STORM OF '87

On Thursday 15th October 1987 BBC TV's weatherman Michael Fish assured the nation that there would be no hurricane. On the morning of Friday 16th October Waldron awoke to a scene of woodland devastation, blocked roads and no power: the hurricane had struck the south of England, leaving electricity and telephone lines down and a trail of destruction in its wake which took days to clear up. John Chambers, Heronsdale Farm, Moat Lane:

> We lost ten acres of softwood, just smashed to matchwood, and eight or nine huge beech trees that were probably a couple of hundred years old, though the chestnut coppice survived. It was three weeks' work to cut up and burn and clear the softwood wreckage. We replanted the whole ten acres with hardwood, mainly oak (about eighty per cent), plus beech and

151

cherry. Twelve years on, the oaks are well-established. The interesting thing is that where we left the woodland to recover by itself, it's probably doing better with self-seeding than the clearance areas: we've got hundreds of birch saplings. Many of the big trees that were lost were very old or rotten, so the storm might have done us all a favour in a way.

Mrs Tutu Whitehead, Danesfield, Moat Lane:

I was terrified because we had so many trees at the side of the house. We had holes in the roof and cypresses lying on the tennis hut. We lost fifty oaks blown over, and about 7,000 Christmas trees and in our twenty-acre wood you couldn't get any sense of direction: it looked as if someone had just trodden on it. The chestnuts and red oaks both survived but it was a scene of almost total destruction on Friday morning. We walked up the road to the Armstrongs next door and it took us twenty minutes to reach them because we had to climb over and round so many fallen trees. We had no telephone or electricity for three weeks, and we moved into the cottage and lit the Rayburn. English Woodlands came and removed the wreckage, and took away 400 tons of fallen larch: we were paid £1 per ton!

Carol Trimbee, Knaves Acre, Burnt Oak:

I was all alone and I thought the roof was coming off the house. As it happened, a fir tree fell neatly on the channel between the two peaks of the roof and hardly did any damage. That night, the cat was going mad, and I didn't want to be upstairs, so we cuddled down together downstairs under the duvet. After the storm I cooked on our Aga for everyone up at the (Burnt Oak) Farm for four days, but I couldn't get the car out for ages because we had seven trees down along the lane, and could only get out on foot. We were cut off for a week. The Farrants lost their chickens—they had a chicken house with 400 in it, and it took off in the hurricane and was never seen again.

Judith Clark: Birch Terrace, Hanging Birch Lane:

I remember the silence that following morning when we all woke up, because there were so many trees down no one could drive anywhere. It was about two hours before you heard the first chainsaw starting up, but it was two weeks before we got our electricity back, and by then it had definitely stopped being interesting. The Terrace inhabitants lived like kings off the contents of everyone's deep-freezers, which had to be cooked and eaten before they went off. It was "Oh lovely, smoked salmon again."

Jeremy Coltart, (then Ragged Dog House, Ragged Dog Lane):

We lay in bed listening to the tiles slithering down the roof with the wind reaching a crescendo, then slipping into another gear with a new and terrifying gust. At the height of the storm we could see the electricity poles down the lane arcing with great sparks flying. Suddenly we were puzzled to see lights below. It was only when we got up and opened the front door that we saw, standing on the doorstep, a supply of milk, left by our intrepid milkman. He had come over from Heathfield in the howling wind anxious not to let us down, then on the way back he found Whitehouse Lane was blocked with fallen trees, so he parked the float at the bottom of the hill, got out and walked all the way home. There were 167 trees torn up at Longmead at the top of Ragged Dog Lane, leaving not a single tree standing, while the house was totally undamaged.

In the village, no one was hurt and only one cottage—Victor Cottage—was badly damaged with the bedroom wall collapsing. The main damage was the loss of hundreds of trees.

Morris dancers at the opening of the Waldron 800 celebrations.

WALDRON 800

It was in 1195 that Bartholomew was appointed the first rector at All Saints' church in Waldron, proof positive that there has been a church and a Christian community in this small village for at least eight centuries. It was an anniversary that could not pass unnoticed and in 1994 our present rector, Roy Greenland, called together a committee, some from within the church community and others from outside it, to put on a celebratory programme.

It wasn't to be just a celebration, however, for Waldron 800 had a specific task to perform: to raise money to support the ministry in our parish beyond the turn of the century. The church commissioners had given notice to every parish that from that date, they would cease to provide their former level of funding for clergy pay, and Waldron 800 was to kick-start a special fund to maintain the future clergy and keep open the churches.

Even those who never went inside the church doors were clear that its role

Sue and Barry Russell, exhibition of Waldron's history, the Old School House.

Presentation of the Ray Pettit cup to Rupert Simmons (Secretary) and Tim Brocklehurst (Captain), celebrity cricket match.

in the village was still important and that everything should be done to ensure its continuation. Plans were put in place for a big weekend of events from 21st-23rd July 1995, with other fundraising events taking place during May and June.

Several gardens were opened one Saturday afternoon in May and the fundraising began. A 'Great Waldron Walk' was organised across the South Downs Way at the beginning of June and, despite foul wet weather, dozens of enthusiastic walkers completed the trek and raised substantial amounts of money for the fund. A jazz evening was held at Bryckden Place. Gay Biddlecombe produced a special white wine with a Waldron 800 label and for every bottle sold, the Waldron 800 fund benefited.

A group of Americans from Texas booked a holiday in Waldron for the big weekend in July through the good offices of John Bowker and Sussex Heritage Holidays, a company which specialises in bringing together people from parishes on either side of the Atlantic. Staying with families in the village the American party spent a week enjoying what Waldron had to offer, exploring our corner of south-east England and finding a warmer welcome than in any hotel, however big and grand.

On the July weekend, a concert by the Heathfield Choral Society with guest soloist Susan McCulloch and the Little London Trio started the celebrations. It was followed by a flower festival, a celebrity cricket match, and

Flower Festival.

a splendid craft and food fair which spilled out into the vineyard, the village street and the recreation ground and included a street band and morris dancers.

There was an historical exhibition at the School House, an art exhibition in the Lucas Hall, a barn dance and barbecue at The Star and on Sunday an outdoor jazz concert which had every foot tapping in the village. A special service was held in All Saints' with guest preacher Bishop Christopher Luxmore. Decorating the pillars in the church was a series of shields, painted by local artist Karen Simmons and her team, illustrating each century of the existence of All Saints'.

At the end of it all, the village had celebrated not only the 800th anniversary, but had also rediscovered its community spirit. There was a warm feeling of commitment to a common goal shared by every single member of the village community—and the celebrations in 1995 had raised some £40,000 for the Waldron 800 fund. The following year, a summer ball and another Great Waldron Walk bolstered the fund towards £60,000.

It was to take five years of interminable discussions before the diocesan authorities and the lawyers had finished tinkering with the fine print to set up a charitable trust, but in the year 2000, finally and at last, the village has had its Waldron 800 fund properly constituted—just in time for the Millennium Festival.

The Great Waldron Walk, 1996.

Harvesting, Heronsdale Farm, summer 1999.

WALDRON'S FARMERS: FACING AN UNCERTAIN FUTURE?

Sixty years ago Britain's farmers were central to the war effort, making the country self-sufficient in essential food. By the end of the twentieth century, the picture had radically changed and, like many others in the agricultural industry, Waldron's farmers were feeling that their whole way of life was under threat.

With the pound at an all-time high, supermarkets driving harder and harder bargains on buying from the farmer, the Common Agricultural Policy (CAP) in the midst of major reform and food scares like BSE changing the eating habits of the western world, the small farmer was at the wrong end of the financial results for at least a decade. Farm incomes halved during 1998, one in twelve farming jobs were lost in the same year and family farmers were giving up the unequal struggle to survive.

As the twentieth century drew to a close, Mike and Doreen Farrant and

159

The Farrant family. Left to right: Stephen with daughter Lucy, Mike and Martin.

their two sons Martin and Steve decided that their family farm at Burnt Oak could no longer support them, and that they would sell off their dairy herd and their milk quota in mid-2000. Their decision meant that after seventy years and four generations, no more daily milk collections would be made from the Farrant farm gate.

Mike said: "The price of milk has gone down by 8.5p per litre in four years. We get 10p a pint, it retails for 25p in the supermarket and 40p on the doorstep. It's not sustainable for us to go on subsidising the consumer." The Farrants hope to stay on their land, but the buildings could become offices and storage for caravans, if planning permission is forthcoming.

Meanwhile the Chambers family at Heronsdale were cautious regarding the future. "Ask me again in a year" said son Matt,

but things have got to get better if we're to go on. There are some promising signs—like the fact that beef consumption has risen back up to

John Chambers.

and beyond what it was when the BSE crisis was at its worst. The future has to include even more co-operative work between farmers. But we're no longer under our own control. The CAP governs how and where we plant our crops, the subsidies have an effect on what we grow and the advent of Eastern European countries into the EU [European Union] could drive more of us out of business. They can buy equipment cheaper and their labour costs are lower.

John Chambers noted the cost of higher standards of hygiene and record keeping in the UK industry, and said that the pressures were getting to many farmers:

It was different fifty years ago when there were more people employed on farms and you could chew things over with other people. Now with increased mechanisation and computerisation, it can be a very lonely business being a farmer, stuck away on a combine out in the fields with nothing but your cab radio and a mobile phone. It's no wonder with all the pressure that farming has one of the highest suicide rates in the country.

The Williams family at Silveroaks, Moat Lane, also decided in 2000 that they couldn't go on with rearing pigs. At the age of thirty-four Kenton Williams was looking at a bleak future:

According to the experts, by the middle of this year 50 per cent of pig producers will have gone out of business. My father's at retirement age and we're ceasing production. It's not what I expected when I came into farming, and I don't think the industry will exist soon, at least not as we know it.

The Delves family at Burnthouse Farm, Lions Green were cautiously upbeat about their continuing future in dairy farming. Andy Delves joked,

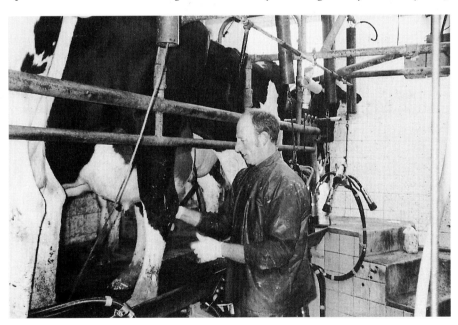

Andy Delves milking the Burjack Herd at Burnt House Farm.

"Not all the dinosaurs went at the same time—some of them hung on for a bit!" He reflected that over the last twenty years of the 20th century the farm had increased its herd from fifty-five cows in 1976 to 160 milking cows and their followers in 2000. They had tried beef and sheep, but found that profit margins were so narrow as to be unsustainable in the longterm. Andy estimated that they would need to increase the herd further to about 200 to stay in business and were planning to invest £30,000 in a newer milking parlour to speed up milking to cope with the increase in numbers.

He commented:

> The milk industry is confused and fragmented at the moment and it's difficult to see quite what the future holds. I think there's still a living to be made in dairying, but you have to be ready to cut costs. It's not easy because the supermarkets tell us that customers are getting more demanding over things like traceability, which puts up the cost of our paperwork, but at the same time they want to reduce the price to the customer. You have to be a serious optimist these days to stay in dairying!

The Bignells at Foxhunt Green will continue, said Paddy Bignell. "The boys [Dennis and Thomas] want to carry on and I've been in farming all my life," she said. They have sheep and some suckler cows and grow corn to feed their own stock.

John Dewe at Tanyard Farm sees some cause for cautious optimism, having just sold some beef cattle at a reasonable price. He intends to continue in farming, being careful, he said "not to put all your eggs in one basket." As well as his beef cattle he will continue with his hay, and has some "do it yourself" liveries for local horse owners. But his dairy cows went two years ago and he feels that it will only be the larger herds which can stay in the milking business with another price cut due in April 2000.

So, as the new century begins, major changes in rural life are being signalled. A leaked government report offers contentious proposals which are expected to cause a furore amongst those who live and work in the countryside. Included are ideas for a tourism tax and the relaxation of tight planning controls.

"The presumption within national policy against development of the best and most versatile land should be removed," the report's writers say. Such a change would have a major impact in the south-east and in particularly desirable areas like Waldron, possibly releasing land to accommodate official targets for new homes. The Ministry of Agriculture could lose the veto over the development of prime farming land, and farmers could be encouraged to sell up or develop new homes, holiday villages and leisure amenities and apply for a change of use of farm buildings to more commercial purposes. Whatever the outcome, it is almost certain that the countryside around Waldron will look radically different in twenty years.

Through the centuries, the countryside has changed and changed again to meet the demands of the day, and farmers have always been ready to adapt. But at the beginning of the twenty-first century, the future of the agricultural industry in the village has never looked more unsure.

Wendy Keyte, summer 1999.

THE LAST VILLAGE SHOPKEEPER

Throughout the last twenty years of the twentieth century, Waldron could support only one general store and post office. Mr Payne ran it for some years in the 1970s and 80s, remembered for his flashes of lugubrious humour ("A little Comfort madam? Certainly, ha ha") followed by Mr and Mrs Broad who barely stayed long enough to make an impact. The last village shopkeeper was Wendy Keyte who became an important personality in the village and tried as hard as anyone could to make the shop a viable proposition over her nine years' tenure.

She ran the post office efficiently, supplied newspapers and had a licence to sell liquor. She stocked all the staple groceries and fresh fruit and vegetables and a range of interesting locally-produced items like cheeses, honey and eggs. For a time the village even had its own sausages, christened "Waldron Porkies". Local children could buy their sweets from Wendy and have them weighed out from a range of old-fashioned glass jars. If you had any particular dietary needs, Wendy was always prepared to get in the stock, and if you needed your shopping delivered she would arrange it. The Beacon View Stores even won a couple of prizes in Wealden District Council's Best Village Shop competition.

Shops depend on customers, however, and eventually Wendy and husband Robin came to the sad conclusion that the profit margin was too narrow. The last village shop was defeated by the social changes which affected many others like it: the movement towards most women going out to work and shopping near their place of employment, and the habit of buying everything at a supermarket. The shop closed on 13th July 1999.

Left to right: Pat Huggins, Beryl Reynolds and Wendy Keyte.

Women's Institute, Millennium Tree Planting: Diana Francis, Rupert Simmons, Ivy Sharpe, Joan Slade, Janet Bonner, Jill Hedley (Secretary), Rita Chant, Barbara Clark (President), Colin Tatt, Betty-Jean Paul, Doreen Freshwater (Treasurer), Liz Scruby, Diane Theis, Pearl Chittleborough, Iris Newson, Sheila Thompson, Dulcie Scott

WALDRON TODAY

Waldron Cricket Club, 2000: Back row: Robin Jackson (President), Quentin Soucek, Jason Simpson, Kevin Taylor, Charlie Huntington, Chris Sargeant, Jonathan Butcher, Rupert Simmons (Secretary). Front row: Vince Miles, Tim Brocklehurst (Chairman) Matthew Chambers (Captain) Jamie Marchant, Mowbray Jackson.

Tony Jarvis,
the village milkman.

Village bus service, three
times a week.

Lynn Seymour,
Waldron's postwoman.

Centre: Donald Chidson (the Party-Giver). Right: Sir Roger Neville (The Knight) with Charles Hendy, prospective parliamentary candidate, at Donald's 80th birthday party at The Star

VILLAGE PERSONALITIES 2000

It's sometimes said that "they don't make the village characters any more", but dig a little deeper and you find . . .

The Deputy Groundsman

A man driven by the ambition to achieve the best and truest village cricket square in Sussex, Mason Scott spends hour upon loving hour, early till late, rolling and cutting Waldron's turf, getting up early to check it on the morning of a match and watching its progress like a mother with a new baby. Famous for putting down tiger droppings on his newly seeded grass to frighten off marauding rabbits.

The Knight

A quiet and courteous man, Sir Roger Neville is a regular at The Star where his tipple is that old naval favourite, pink gin, which he enjoys without noticeable effect. Endlessly hospitable, he and Lady Neville host a moving population of children, grandchildren, partners and friends at their home. He sponsors an annual cricket match, the Possingworth team v. the Village, followed by a barbecue for all participants at which prodigious amounts of beer evaporate and the hangovers are said to last three days.

Star of The Star

Blonde, blue-eyed, petite and very determined, Lesley Lefort is the power behind husband Paul, publican of The Star Inn. Her fortieth birthday party, held in a marquee in the pub garden, became a village legend when it rained solidly from start to finish, there was as much mud as in a farmyard and ninety dinner jackets went to the local cleaners on the following Monday. She presides regularly over the preparation of hundreds of meals in the Star's kitchen, but off duty, she throws a mean dart and is a devoted mum to Amie, William and George.

The Party-Giver

Donald Chidson collects people as others collect stamps. They are his hobby and men, women and children of all ages are on the receiving end of his bright blue gaze and considerable charm. Argumentative and opinionated, he scarcely missed a beat even when he was hospitalised for a quadruple heart bypass, but returned to the pub on his way home from hospital, to a round of applause. His parties are famous, held at The Star every five years, to which everyone is invited. This year it's his eightieth, and it promises to be quite a celebration.

The Vineyard Owner

Over twenty years Gay Biddlecombe put Waldron in the press and on the map, promoting St George's English wines. She makes no secret of the fact that she prefers animals to people, and wrote a best-selling book about her experiences in Waldron which amused, intrigued and offended the residents in almost equal measure.

Centre: Monique Gray (The Judge). Right: Dr Pieter Gray (The Doc)

The Doc

Pieter Gray presided over the health of Waldron's residents for thirty years as their GP, working devotedly seven days a week, twenty-four hours a day. Known and loved by several generations as "Doc", his modesty and diffidence explained his smiling comment when referring a patient to a consultant: "I'm going to send you to a proper doctor."

The best kind of GP and a student of the human race, in retirement he has tended his vines and become an accomplished cook.

The Judge

One of England's first women circuit judges, Monique Gray (Viner) managed that difficult juggling act of combining a career in the law with having four children. A formidable personality with a piercing and challenging gaze, she is also a fiercely competitive tennis player, a competent musician, enthusiastic traveller and excellent conversationalist. Woe betide anyone who opens their mouth without having a clear idea of what they want to say.

The Volunteers

Villages need their willing volunteers and Waldron is lucky in having a large number who quietly go about making things happen. It's impossible to name them all, but just three examples picked at random to represent the others are Christopher Corfield, Roy Wilkinson and Di Chapman. Christo is a staunch regular and sidesman at church, a member of its finance committee trying to make ends meet. He broadcasts regularly for the Wealden Talking Newspapers charity and is involved in more associations and societies than most of us have even heard of. Roy is seen everywhere on his beloved bike, and is always willing to help organise events, source supplies of necessary equipment, direct traffic, operate as a practical handyman, and even pick up litter down the lane past his home. He's famous for being the only male involved with the WI market. Wife Mary is the inventor of our Snowdrop Mile and a Women's Institute member. Di helped to run a notably successful campaign to keep open the village school for several years in the 1960s, and these days leads the team of flower arrangers who make the church beautiful week after week and put on our biennial flower festival.

The Wafflers

With elbows on the bar and glasses in hand, the lunchtime Wafflers tell stories, compare experiences and set the world to rights with opinions which sometimes would horrify Attila the Hun. Of the regulars, Jack Armstrong is a stand-up comedian *manqué* who can tell jokes for up to an hour without repeating himself. The next generation (The Young Wafflers) meet at The Star on Tuesday evening (after the children are in bed) and are in training for when their turn comes to reorder the world.

The High Sheriff

Alan Mays Smith is large in every sense of the word, in voice, appearance and personality and was an oarsman in his university days. He had a notably successful spell as high sheriff of East Sussex in 1995-96 when the world came to Waldron. He is enormously supportive of all village events, a worker for good causes, chairman of the Neighbourhood Watch and a generous host with his wife Rosemary.

The Cricket Lover

The only personality who is no more, but it's still worth mentioning Les Crapper who was a regular at The Star for years. He also enjoyed his pint at The Six Bells, Chiddingly and The Yew Tree at Chalvington, so when he went to the great hostelry in the sky his family presented a trophy for the three pub cricket teams to contest in a limited-overs, knockout competition. Not a cup or shield, but a tastefully mounted tin potty with, painted on the side, a seated cricketer in his whites, contemplating his future.

The Village Policeman

Brian Tompsett was Waldron's village policeman for years and although now retired, he still lives on the patch. Knows more about the old times than anyone, and is the moving force who organises the reunions for those who went to the village school. A quiet operator, he's often seen cycling round the lanes and is always ready to help with village projects.

The Cyclist

Sixteen-year-old Keith Newsam from North Street has been a leading competitive road racing cyclist for several years, achieving success and recognition at national level. He is that rarity, someone who has known where he wants to go from an early age. His determination to win takes him out training in all weathers, and while he is still at school he works in village gardens to earn money to support his hobby. If any of Waldron's current crop of young people are to become nationally famous, it could be Keith.

The Churchwarden

All Saints' is very lucky to have a devoted churchwarden in Ruth Challis. Her duties include looking after the fabric of the church and taking responsibility for anything from the boiler to the trees in the churchyard. Needs great tact and persuasiveness to juggle the competing demands of the village, the congregation, the parochial church council and the diocese and manages them all with quiet authority. She also sings in the choir and is a school governor at Cross-in-Hand Church of England Primary School.

The Farmer

There have been Chambers at Heronsdale Manor since the 1930s and John Chambers has lived there all his life. His knowledge of the village's recent history is prodigious and he plays a very full part in Waldron's community life, offering practical help in village events, being a regular sidesman at church, a parish councillor, and having had several years as a well-respected chairman of the Waldron Cricket Club. Something of a philosopher, he recognises but doesn't resent the changes he sees all around him in farming and in village life. Wife Dawn and son Matt are also closely involved in village affairs.

The Man of Waldron

There aren't many in the village now who are Waldron born and bred but Robin Hunnisett is one. Born in Warren Lane in 1927, he was brought up and educated in the village, attending the village school until he was fourteen. He worked on farms around the village, was a member of the Home Guard during World War Two, was a times Secretary of the cricket club and a bell-ringer, and only moved away in 1951 when he married. Father Alec was a stalwart of the village's football and cricket teams both before and after the War. Robin still owns a five-acre patch of land on the edge of the village in Whitehouse Lane, where he has created a small plantation of hardwoods and pines. He tends them with loving care, visiting them on most days in the year and brewing up in his little barn. His greatest ambition is to return to Waldron and he still feels his roots are here.

Waldron Millennium Festival Committee. Left to right: Mary Wilkinson, Pat Nichols, Valerie Chidson (Chairman), Barbara Clark, John Heywood (Treasurer), Dianne Steele, Gill Temple, Vanessa Bertram, Rog Carmichael, Diane Caird. Not shown: Judith Clark, Jeremy Coltart, Jean Paul, Alan Parnell, Sarah Porpora.

THE WALDRON MILLENNIUM FESTIVAL

In early 1998 a questionnaire went round to all the households on Waldron's electoral register, asking if anyone wanted to celebrate the year 2000, and if so, how? The form also gave an opportunity for volunteers to come forward to help on an organising committee or in practical ways like typing, baking, marshalling, car parking, delivering newsletters, putting up posters or manning stalls.

Once the returns had been analysed, thirteen people who had volunteered to go on the organising committee met to work out a programme. Requests for events were so various that it was immediately obvious there was more than could possibly be crammed into one weekend. So the concept of the Waldron

Millennium Festival was born, with an ambitious list of events spread over ten days.

Most often requested was a historical exhibition or a display of old photographs of the village. Sue and Barry Russell offered to arrange this from their vast collection of Waldron memorabilia, and from the early discussions came the idea of a book which would be something more permanent for every resident after the Festival was over. A record of all those living in the village on 1st January 2000 was carried out amongst those on the November 1999 electoral register for Waldron, so that the present-day villagers could have their names recorded in the book. Over ninety-two per cent of householders returned their forms and the results appear at the end of this section.

Another frequent request was for events which would involve the children. So two performances of Benjamin Britten's *Noye's Fludde* went into the programme, a village fête was planned to open the whole Festival and a village picnic party with crazy sports for all was lined up to finish it. The flower festival team offered to time their display at All Saints' to coincide with the Millennium Festival celebrations, and the local sketch club planned an exhibition. Jazz, opera and folk music all had their devotees, and went into the programme which was beginning to look very ambitious and expensive.

To finance the plans, the committee started a Friends of Waldron Millennium Festival Association, asking everyone for a subscription of £15, in return for which came priority booking privileges and reduced ticket prices. Patronage and sponsorship was sought from individual people, local businesses, Wealden District Council and the Millennium Festival Awards for All (national) Fund. By the end of February 2000, a total of 162 households had joined the Friends, the Awards for All scheme had grant-aided us, as had Wealden District Council and a number of generous local people and businesses. Several successful fundraising events were held to finance the Festival, and the cost of putting it on began to look manageable.

Keeping in touch with everyone in the village became an important priority and a quarterly (later monthly) newsletter was circulated, printed on paper supplied by a resident. The advance booking form, designed by another resident, was circulated in January and February to the village and went on general public release in March. Volunteers to give the Lucas Hall a lick of paint were asked for and a working weekend planned.

Extra ideas which could not be packed into the ten days of the Festival itself were arranged in a "Festival Fringe." A mile of snowdrops was planted over two autumns which resulted in a splendid display in January. A Bluebell Walk in May 2000 was planned, as well as an open-air performance of *Two Gentlemen of Verona* in August and an exhibition called "Mapping the Millennium" also in that month.

As this book goes to press, expectations are running high and all the planning is reaching a final conclusion, with artists booked, canvas and loos rented, applications for certificates or licences made, souvenir mugs ordered, a souvenir programme in preparation, and an exhausted but exhilarated committee working themselves into a fever. Anyone who says community spirit is dead should see the list of people who have pulled their weight already or have volunteered to help during the Festival itself. All that is needed now is fine weather.

The children rehearsing Noye's Fludde.

THE WALDRON RECORD 2000

When this book was in the planning stage, the authors wanted to make it a celebration of the history of Waldron, a source of pleasure and a souvenir of the year 2000 for present and past village residents. They also had an ambition to make it a unique source of information for future local historians and people researching their families.

To do that, they proposed a voluntary mini-census, a record of every person living in the village at the turn of the century, on the first day of January 2000. Between Christmas 1999 and New Year a letter went out to all households on the Waldron electoral register, asking for the co-operation of everyone and enclosing a table to fill in. Between 1st January and 29th February over ninety-two per cent of these forms was returned, giving a unique and remarkably complete profile of Waldron at the turn of the century. Those few who chose not to return their form have still been listed, but only with the bare name details which appear in the electoral register.

The results were compared with those of the census of 1851. The two showed that there had been a complete change of lifestyle and population in the intervening century and a half and the figures which follow demonstrate the change.

The Areas Covered

It was not possible to replicate exactly the areas covered in both surveys. For the Record 2000, only those households which are listed in the present Waldron electoral register were included. The roads and lanes are Back Lane (south, as far as the New Pond Hill turning), Brittenden Lane, Burnt Oak Lane, Cambridge

Lane, Dern Lane (part), Firgrove Road, Forest Place, Foxhunt Green, Hanging Birch Lane as far as Leopards Mill, the High Street, Hollow Lane, Lions Green, Moat Lane, North Street, Possingworth Road, Ragged Dog Lane, Rosers Cross, the centre of Waldron, Warren Close, Warren Lane and Whitehouse Lane.

From the 1851 census the registration district described as Framfield South was used for comparison: "All that part of the parish that lies on the South side of the high road leading from Black Boys to Horeham [sic] as far as Hooks Farm including all the houses adjoining that road, likewise all those comprising the village of Waldron".

This gave us 306 households and 730 people for the Record 2000, and for the 1851 census, 297 people within a catchment area roughly similar.

Ages

Surprisingly, present-day Waldron has no less than 124 children of fourteen and under, with 143 at school or university. Compare that with 1851, and we see that only eighteen went to school even though the *Parliamentary Gazette* of 1843-44 reported of Waldron that "Here in this Parish there is a day school". Education was still not free for all, however, and children were regarded as useful labour on farms and in the house.

The age profile was completely different between the two surveys (see Fig. 1). The 1851 survey started high with a majority of under tens, and steadily reduced in a straight line to the over eighty-year olds of whom Waldron had only four. For the year 2000, the numbers climb steeply for the first two decades, then drop dramatically for the next two before climbing steeply again as the forty to sixty year-olds buy into the village, presumably with greater disposable income.

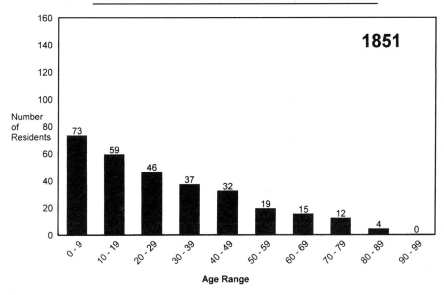

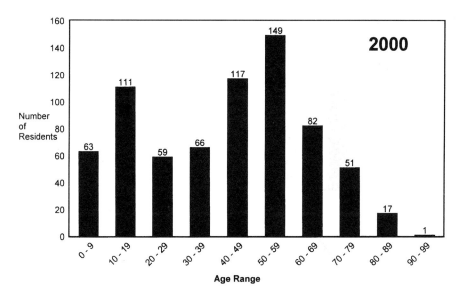

Figs. 1a & b. Age Range

The Biggest Changes

The most obvious changes are seen in the comparison of the size of families, the places of birth (see Fig.2) and the occupations (see Fig.3). In 1851 the size of household averaged out at 5.8 people, while in 2000 it is 2.6, with households of six being a rarity.

In 1851 the vast majority of Waldron's villagers were born and stayed in the village. Today's residents come from all over the UK but with hospital births being the norm, the figures are skewed since many of the village's young people cite Eastbourne or Pembury, Kent, as their birthplace, the locations of the two maternity hospitals serving the area. In 1851 there was only one person born outside the UK living in the village, but today there are no less than forty-six born overseas (see Fig.2).

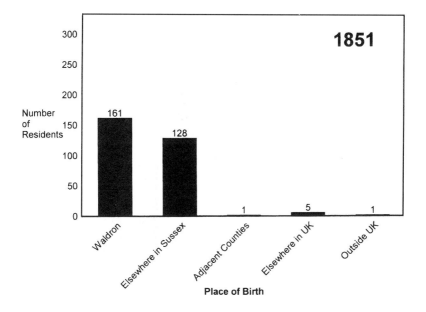

Fig. 2a Place of Birth

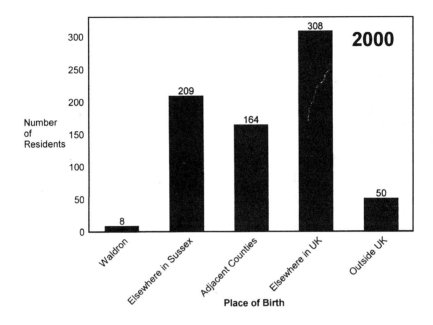

Fig. 2b Place of Birth

The most frequently cited occupations in 1851 were either agricultural or connected with the farming industry (see Fig 3). In 2000, agriculture still makes a showing, but it is only given by thirty-five people as their occupation. It is no surprise to see the greater spread of professions and occupations in 2000, reflecting more choice in work options. Not including women who described themselves as housewives, there were eighty-one people who declared that they worked from home, indicating perhaps a growing trend for home working in the computer age. In 1851 the options for most villagers were working on the land, staying at home to have children or going into service.

In social status, no one in 2000 describes themselves either as a pauper or a gentleman, but in 1851 Waldron had nine paupers and two gentlemen!

One question was asked in 2000 about car ownership which did not appear in 1851 for obvious reasons. The number of cars per household today averaged out at 2.0, reflecting the greater mobility of the population in the automobile era and the sad lack of public transport in rural areas today.

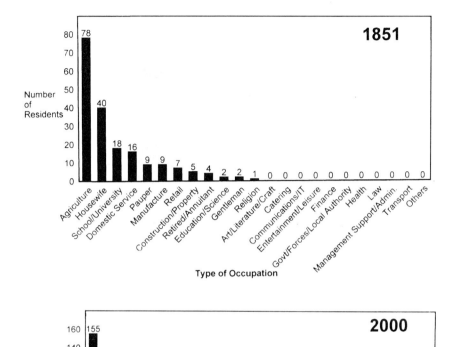

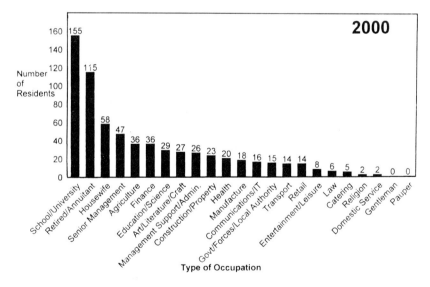

Figs. 3a & b Occupations

THE FULL RECORD

It was not possible to include all the individual details of our Waldron Record 2000 in this book, nor would it necessarily have been desirable. The compilers were, however, keen to have a full record kept in a safe place for future local historians and genealogists to consult so a full set of the survey results will be lodged with the Sussex Record Society and a second set with the church records. Today's villagers are, after all, part of Waldron's long history.

Vanessa Bertram was the computer expert who volunteered to take up the challenge of inputting all the records, preparing the analytical figures and making comparisons with the 1851 census returns.

Name	Occupation	Place of Birth
Adamson, Ian	Chartered Engineer	Bolton, Lancashire
Aldrich, Catherine	Secretary	Dublin, Eire
Aldrich, David	Retired Fire Brigade Officer	London
Alexander, Kate	Teacher	Yeovil, Somerset
Allchorn, Geoffrey	Company Director	Eastbourne, East Sussex
Allchorn, Helen	Sales Executive	Cuckfield, West Sussex
Allchorn, Olivia		Eastbourne, East Sussex
Amies, Mary	Retired	Wilmington, Kent
Anderson, Elizabeth		
Anderson, James		
Anderson, Victoria		
Anniss, Jane	Horticulturist	Selsey, West Sussex
Anniss, John	Antiques Restorer	Westcliffe-on-Sea, Essex
Anthony, Jane	Housewife	Great Yarmouth, Norfolk
Aris, Adrian		Woking, Surrey
Armstrong, Felicity	Housewife	Watford, Northants
Armstrong, John	Retired	Newcastle, Northumberland
Ashwell, Caroline	Housewife	Pembury, Kent
Ashwell, George	Student	Pembury, Kent
Ashwell, Stephen	Underwriter	Chigwell, Essex
Ashwell, Thomas	Student	London
Atkinson, Caroline	Director Software Company	Beckenham, Kent
Atkinson, Keisey		Eastbourne, East Sussex
Atkinson, Kevin	Farm Manager	Ashford, Kent
Atkinson, Shannon		Ashford, Kent
Atkinson, Sharon	Housewife	London
Baker, Barbara		Wells, Somerset
Baker, Ben		Pembury, Kent
Baker, Charles		
Baker, Christine	School Care Officer	Haveluy, France
Baker, David	Student	Pembury, Kent
Baker, Denise	Nursery Assistant/Mother	Greenwich, London

Name	Occupation	Place of Birth
Baker, Margaret		
Baker, Matthew	Student	Pembury, Kent
Baker, Rowan	Student	Eastbourne, East Sussex
Baker, Sarah	Student	Pembury, Kent
Baker, Simon	Retired	Hove, East Sussex
Baker, Sydney	Retired Dental Surgeon	London
Baker, Trevor	Communications Manager	Lewisham, London
Baldwin, Sam	Student	Tunbridge Wells, Kent
Baldwin, Vivien		Caterham, Surrey
Bannister, Alistair	Farmer	Brighton, East Sussex
Bannister, Christopher	Farmer	Seaford, East Sussex
Bannister, Emma	Publican	Brighton, East Sussex
Bannister, Jean	Farmer/Housewife	Seaford, East Sussex
Barton, Amanda	Student	Eastbourne, East Sussex
Barton, Elizabeth	Homemaker	Lewes, East Sussex
Barton, John	Carpenter/Painter/Decorator	Blackboys, East Sussex
Barton, Lydia	Student	Eastbourne, East Sussex
Barton, Sarah	Student	Eastbourne, East Sussex
Bartup, Norman	Sales Manager	Brighton, East Sussex
Bartup, Paul	Lorry Driver	Portsmouth, Hampshire
Bartup, Valerie	Housewife	Eastbourne, East Sussex
Bather, Alison	Secretary/ Housewife	East Grinstead, West Sussex
Bather, Robin	Management Consultant	Fulmer, Buckinghamshire
Beatson, Dan	Student	London
Beatson, John	Civil Engineer	Waipawa, New Zealand
Beatson, Lydia	Student	Eastbourne, East Sussex
Beatson, Vicki	Writer/Editor	Suva, Fiji
Beeney, Charlotte	Student	Eastbourne, East Sussex
Beeney, Jonathon	Manager Healthcare	Eastbourne, East Sussex
Beeney, Stella	Mailing House Assistant	Crowborough, East Sussex
Begg, Angus		Tunbridge Wells, Kent
Begg, Donald	Lloyd's Broker	Lima, Peru
Begg, Emma	Student	London
Begg, Katie	Student	London
Begg, Nicola		Exeter, Devon
Bench, Joy	Housewife	Hambrook, Bristol
Bench, Philip	Retired	Maidenhead, Berkshire
Bennett, Carol	Dancer	Warlingham, Surrey
Bennett, Charlie	Businessman	London
Bennett, Christine	Homemaker	Morecambe, Lancashire
Bennett, Clare		Pembury, Kent
Bennett, Daniel		Brighton, East Sussex
Bennett, Juliet	Marketing Account Manager	London
Bennett, Leonie		Brighton, East Sussex
Bennett, Raymond	Lawyer	Tonbridge, Kent
Biddlecombe, Gay	Vineyard Owner/Journalist	South Shields, County Durham
Biddlecombe, Peter	Business Consultant/Author	London
Bignell, Dennis	Farmer/Contractor	Ashford, Kent
Bignell, Patricia	Farmer/Housewife	Hastings, East Sussex
Bignell, Thomas	Student	Ashford, Kent

Name	Occupation	Place of Birth
Birkett, Annella	Student	Manchester, Lancashire
Birkett, John	Retired	London
Black, Antony	Engineer	Farnborough, Kent
Black, Lyndsay	TV Assistant Producer	Farnborough, Kent
Black, Mary	Publishing	Farnborough, Kent
Black, Stuart	Scientist	Farnborough, Kent
Bonney, Charles	Sales Manager	Carshalton, Surrey
Bonney, Karen	Reflexologist	Meopham, Kent
Bonney, Lucy		Eastbourne, East Sussex
Bonney, Nicola	Student	Eastbourne, East Sussex
Bourne, Andrew	Student	Exeter, Devon
Bourne, Carolyn	Company Director	Brighton, East Sussex
Bourne, Geoffrey	Farmer	Moreton-in-Marsh, Glos.
Bowe, Peter	Project Bid Manager	Liverpool, Merseyside
Bowring, Edgar	Retired Company Director	
Brady, Richard		
Braham, Albert	Graphic Designer	London
Braham, Maureen	Housewife	London
Brererton, Stamatia		
Brereton, Daphne		
Brewer, Patricia		Clifton, Somerset
Broad, Evelyn	Student	Eastbourne, East Sussex
Broad, Jenny	Housewife	Crowborough, East Sussex
Broad, Jonathan	Student	Camberley, Surrey
Broad, Roy	Airline Pilot	Moreton-in-Marsh, Glos.
Brown, Alexander	Student	Brighton, East Sussex
Brown, Anthony		
Brown, Ashley	Chartered Town Planner	Crawley, West Sussex
Brown, Duncan	Student	Brighton, East Sussex
Brown, Hilary	Housewife/Speech Therapist	Enfield, London
Brown, Lesley		
Brownbridge, Carly	Student	Pembury, East Sussex
Brownbridge, Jessica	Student	Pembury, East Sussex
Brownbridge, Katherine		Pembury, East Sussex
Brownbridge, Richard	Builder	Carlton, Yorkshire
Brownbridge, Ruth	Teacher	Rustington, West Sussex
Burgess, Emily	Student	Eastbourne, East Sussex
Burgess, Jeff	Garage Proprietor	Eastbourne, East Sussex
Burgess, Nina	Housewife	Heathfield, East Sussex
Burgess, Roland	Retired	Blackboys, East Sussex
Burgess, Sue	Housewife	Ross-on-Wye, Hereford
Burrett, Elaine		
Butler, Stephan	Director	Wisbech, Cambridgeshire
Caird, Charles	Retired	Middlesborough, Nrthmbrlnd
Caird, Diane	Deputy Registrar	Hayes, Middlesex
Callender, Margaret		
Cameron, Diana	Retired Housewife/Teacher	Broseley, Salop
Cameron, Peter	Retired Bank Director	Calcutta, India
Cardell, Anne	Retired	Monaghan, Monaghan
Cardell, Brian	Retired	Stockport, Cheshire

Name	Occupation	Place of Birth
Carmichael, Michael	Retired	Blackheath, Middlesex
Carter, John	Retired	London, Surrey
Carter, Susan	Retired	Edgware, Middlesex
Chadwick, Yvonne		
Chambers, Dawn	Housewife	Eastbourne, East Sussex
Chambers, Hannah	Student	Farnborough, Kent
Chambers, Sidney	Artist	West Malling, Kent
Chambers, William	Farmer	Lambeth, London
Chambers, William	Farmer	Eastbourne, East Sussex
Chapman, Allan	Retired	Lions Green, East Sussex
Chapman, Charlotte		Cross-in-Hand, East Sussex
Chapman, Dinah	Housewife	Newark-on-Trent, Notts.
Chapman, Graham	Product Manager	Sheffield, Yorkshire
Chapman, Hannah	Student	Eastbourne, East Sussex
Chapman, Karen	Air Stewardess	Pembury, Kent
Chapman, Rebekah		Eastbourne, East Sussex
Chidson, Donald	Retired Director General	Gillingham, Kent
Chidson, Valerie	PR Consultant	Brighton, East Sussex
Chisnall, Andrew	Underwriter/Manager	Tunbridge Wells, Kent
Chisnall, Laura	Secretary	Enfield, Middlesex
Chittleburgh, Pearl	Retired	Ilford, Essex
Chittleburgh, William	Retired	London
Clare, John	Antiques Dealer	London, Essex
Clare, June Ann		London, Middlesex
Clark, Barbara	District Councillor	Matlock, Derbyshire
Clark, John	Consultant	London
Clark, Judith	Artistic Director	Burnley, Lancashire
Clark, Lorna	Student	Eastbourne, East Sussex
Clark, Paul	Retailer	Sutton, Surrey
Clark, Sandra	Retailer	Brighton, East Sussex
Clayton-Smith, Anna	Student	London
Clayton-Smith, Ian	Company Director	London
Clayton-Smith, Lynda	Lettings Negotiator	Whitehaven, Cumbria
Cleary, Margaret	Open University Student	Cheam, Surrey
Clue, Abigail	Student	Wolverhampton, West Mids.
Clue, Adam	Student	Bristol, Avon
Clue, Roger	Chief Executive	Southsea, Hampshire
Clue, Sheila	Housewife	London
Clutton, Jo	Teacher	London
Clutton, Laura	PR Consultant	Grantham, Lincolnshire
Clutton, Nicholas	Pilot	Dallington, East Sussex
Cockerill, Robert	Retired	London
Coleman, Derek		
Coles, Simon	Chartered Accountant	Bromley, Kent
Collins, Charlotte		Eastbourne, East Sussex
Collins, Lin	Mother	Eastbourne, East Sussex
Collins, Peter	Market Maker	Eastbourne, East Sussex
Collins, Samuel		Eastbourne, East Sussex
Colliss, Carrie	Marketing Manager	Andover, Hampshire
Coltart, Jeremy	Insurance Broker	Glasgow, Strathclyde

Name	Occupation	Place of Birth
Coltart, Sue	Nursery School Teacher	Hindhead, Surrey
Cook, Violet	Retired	Newcastle, Northumberland
Cooper, Marie		Harrogate, Yorkshire
Corfield, Christopher	Stockbroker	Redruth, Cornwall
Corfield, Michael	Company Director	Battle, East Sussex
Corfield, Philippa	Theatrical Costumier	Glasgow, Strathclyde
Corfield, Rachael	Student Nurse	Nakuru, Kenya
Coster, Chloe	Property Developer	Woodford, Essex
Coster, Holly-Louise	Student	Cuckfield, West Sussex
Coster, Josiah	Student	Douglas, Isle of Man
Coster, Michael	Quantity Surveyor	Eastbourne, East Sussex
Court, Alan	Consulting Engineer	Eastbourne, East Sussex
Court, Betty	Retired	Rye, East Sussex
Court, Jennifer	Teacher	Crowborough, East Sussex
Cousley, Allen	Retired	Moneymore, Co. Londonderry
Cousley, Audrie	Practice Nurse	Londonderry, Co. Londonderry
Cousley, Roz	Student	Newtownards, Co. Down
Cox, Paul	Builder	Sutton Coldfield, Warwickshire
Cragg, Benedict	Student	London
Cragg, Charlotte	Student	London
Cragg, Michael	Builder	Neath, West Glamorgan
Cragg, Phillippa	Housewife	Bishop Auckland, Durham
Creasey, Jolyon	Property Maintenance	Harlow, Essex
Crook, Alexander	Student	Cuckfield, West Sussex
Crook, Andrea	Potter	London
Crook, Phillip		
Crow, Angela	Retired	Chesterfield, Derbyshire
Crow, Michael	Retired	Wolverhampton, Staffordshire
Davenport Thomas, Caroline	Marketing Executive	London
Davenport Thomas, Jane	Florist	Lichfield, Staffordshire
Davies, Elizabeth		Ipswich, Suffolk
Davis, Clare	Student	Pembury, Kent
Davis, Emma	Student	Eastbourne, East Sussex
Davis, Judith	Pre-school Teacher	Eastbourne, East Sussex
Davis, Peter	Heating Engineer	Eastbourne, East Sussex
Davis, Thomas	Student	Eastbourne, East Sussex
Davis, Valerie	Housewife	Heathfield, East Sussex
Davis, William	Accountant	Eltham, London
Day, Claire	Royal Navy	London
Day, Kevin	Housing Officer	London
Day, Laura	Student	London
Day, Susan	Housing Officer	London
Deadman, Andrew	Director/Manager	Farnborough, Kent
Deadman, Ann	Hairdresser	Kingston-on-Thames, Surrey
Deadman, Bradley	Student	Eastbourne, East Sussex
Deadman, Ryan	Student	Eastbourne, East Sussex
Delves, Andrew	Farmer	Horam, East Sussex
Delves, Elizabeth	Housewife/Teacher	Hammersmith, London
Delves, Hannah	Student	Waldron, East Sussex
Delves, Jethro	Fencer	Waldron, East Sussex

Name	Occupation	Place of Birth
Delves, Joseph	Farmworker	Waldron, East Sussex
Delves, Joyce	Housewife	London, Essex
Delves, Ronald	Farmer	Horam, East Sussex
Denness, Alexander	Student	Cuckfield, West Sussex
Denness, Christian	Student	Eastbourne, East Sussex
Denness, Mona	Retired	Uckfield, East Sussex
Denness, Richard	Builder	Pembury, Kent
Denness, Roland	Retired	Hadlow Down, East Sussex
Denness, Sarah	Housewife	Cuckfield, West Sussex
Denton, Alexandra	Student	Cuckfield, West Sussex
Denton, Geoffrey	Solicitor	Manchester, Lancashire
Denton, Judith	Nursery School Proprietor	Wakefield, Yorkshire
Denton, William	Student	Cuckfield, West Sussex
Dewe, Emma	Student	Eastbourne, East Sussex
Dewe, John	Farmer	Brighton, East Sussex
Dewe, Rebecca	Student	Eastbourne, Sussex
Dexter, Alan	Retired	Peterborough, Northants.
Dexter, Celine	Retired	Clifden, Ireland
Ditchburn, Elizabeth	Systems Development Manager	Winchester, Hampshire
Ditchburn, John	Student	Cuckfield, West Sussex
Ditchburn, John		Morpeth, Northumberland
Ditchburn, Peter	Student	Cuckfield, West Sussex
Dixon, Ann		
Dixon, Carolyn	Catering Assistant	Knebworth, Hertfordshire
Dixon, Ian		
Dixon, Roger	Chartered Accountant	Southsea, Hampshire
Donnachie, Angela	Housewife	Glasgow, Strathclyde
Donnachie, Douglas	Student	Haywards Heath, West Sussex
Donnachie, Frank		Paisley, Renfrewshire
Donnachie, Michelle		Haywards Heath, West Sussex
Driver, Joan		
Driver, Peter		
Duffell, Joy	Housewife	Birmingham, West Midlands
Duffell, Sue	Nurse	Ealing, London
Dupasquier, Philippe	Illustrator	Neuchatel, Switzerland
Dupasquier, Sophie	Student	Eastbourne, East Sussex
Dupasquier, Sylvie	Accountant	Paris, France
Dupasquier, Timothy	Student	Camden, London
Durne, Martin	Telecommunications Consultant	Hammersmith, London
Durne, Vivienne	Budget Analyst	Greenwich, London
Dwyer, Nigel	Salesman	Newquay, Cornwall
Egerton, Mandy	Company Director	Sutton Coldfield, Warwickshire
Ellis, Chloe	Student	Eastbourne, East Sussex
Ellis, Elizabeth	Teacher/Housewife	Newcastle upon Tyne
Elmitt, Caroline	Shop Manager	Bath, Somerset
Elmitt, Michael	Bursar	Swindon, Wiltshire
Eustace, Tim	Businessman	Beddington, Surrey
Evans, Alexandra	Student	Welwyn, Hertfordshire
Evans, Emily		Pembury, Kent
Evans, Florence	Retired	Merthyr Tydfil, Glamorgan

Name	Occupation	Place of Birth
Evans, Jenny		Pembury, Kent
Evans, Joan		Audley, Staffordshire
Evans, John	Psychologist	Brighton, East Sussex
Evans, Lynn	Public Relations Manager	Bromley, Kent
Evans, Michael	Student	Welwyn, Hertfordshire
Evans, Victoria		Seaton, Devon
Evison, Heather	Housewife	Lewisham, London
Evison, Ronald	Retired	Old Coulsdon, Surrey
Fanshawe, Louisa		London
Fanshawe, Maura	Housewife	Upham, Hampshire
Fanshawe, Richard	Marketing Consultant	Hong Kong, Hong Kong
Farrant, Caroline	Mother/Accounts Assistant	Ashurst, Kent
Farrant, Doreen	Dairy Farmer	Cross-in-Hand, East Sussex
Farrant, Lucy		Eastbourne, East Sussex
Farrant, Martin	Farmer	Pembury, East Sussex
Farrant, Michael	Dairy Farmer	Waldron, East Sussex
Farrant, Paul	Student	Eastbourne, East Sussex
Farrant, Stephen	Farmer	Pembury, Kent
Farrant, Vicki	Veterinary Nurse	Eastbourne, East Sussex
Faulkner, Alan	Schools Inspector	Wandsworth, London
Faulkner, Bethan	Student	Eastbourne, East Sussex
Faulkner, Megan	Student	Eastbourne, East Sussex
Faulkner, Neill	Student	Eastbourne, East Sussex
Faulkner, Pamela	Part time Sales Assistant	Castle Donnington, Leics.
Faulkner, Roy	Banker	London
Faulkner, Sian	School Learning Asst.	Merthyr Tydfil, Glamorgan
Feacham, Jennifer		
Ferguson, Mary	Retired	Ealing, Middlesex
Flynn, Irene	Airline Manager	Clifton, Bristol
Francis, Audrey	Artist	Staines, Middlesex
Francis, Owen	Retired Company Secretary	Parkstone, Dorset
Franks, Jake	Student	London, Surrey
Franks, Mary Liz	Graphic Designer	Dublin, Ireland
Franks, Michel	Photographer	Johannesburg, South Africa
Franks, Sophie	Student	London, Surrey
Fraser, John	Retired	Kerang, Australia
Fraser, Lynette	Housewife	Bromley, Kent
Freeman, Colin	Voluntary Worker	Amersham, Buckinghamshire
Freeman, Margaret	Retired Teacher/Voluntary Work	Guildford, Surrey
Freshwater, Doreen	Retired	Stratford, London
Fulljames, Jennifer		
Fulljames, Roger		
Garden, Paul	Control Engineer	Greenwich, London
Garden, Penelope	Student	Eastbourne, East Sussex
Garden, Philippa	Student	Eastbourne, East Sussex
Garden, Susan	Teacher	Douglas, Isle of Man
Gentle, Jeanette	Retired	London
Gentle, John	Retired	London
Gibbons, Catherine	Student	Bedford, Bedfordshire
Gibbons, Roy	Chartered Insurer	Kingston Upon Thames

Name	Occupation	Place of Birth
Gibbons, Wendy	Administrator	Bradford, W. Yorkshire
Gillatt, Betty	Retired	Bromley, Kent
Gillich, Rolf	Decorator	Remscheid, Germany
Gillich, Valerie	Housewife	Bexhill, East Sussex
Gillies, Daisy		Hadlow Down, East Sussex
Gillies, Fred	Plant Fitter	Hadlow Down, East Sussex
Gillies, Louise	Florist/ Housewife	Crowborough, East Sussex
Gingell, Alex	Farmer/Sawyer	Pembury, Kent
Gingell, Edward	Student	Eastbourne, East Sussex
Gingell, Georgina	Teacher's Assistant	Stafford, Staffordshire
Gingell, Harry	Student	Eastbourne, East Sussex
Gingell, Rebecca	Student	Eastbourne, East Sussex
Gould, Patience		
Green, Duncan	Dental Surgeon	Worthing, West Sussex
Greenlees, Camilla	Student	London
Greenlees, Daisy	Student	Eastbourne, East Sussex
Greenlees, Grania	Montessori Teacher	Hong Kong, Hong Kong
Greenlees, Laragh	Artist	Johannesburg, South Africa
Greenlees, Loudon	Stockbroker	London
Greenlees, Rupert	Student	London
Grey, Carolyn	Housewife	Barnet, Hertfordshire
Grey, Monique	Retired Circuit Judge	Brussels, Belgium
Grey, Pieter	Retired G.P.	Antwerp, Belgium
Grey, Robert	Company Director	Orpington, Kent
Griffiths, Sally-Ann	Riding Instructor	Pembury, Kent
Grimsey, Jacqueline	Housewife	Romford, Essex
Grimsey, Ken	Builder & Plumber	Bexleyheath, Kent
Guthrie, Anna	Student	London
Guthrie, Colin	Surveyor	Kingston upon Thames
Guthrie, Elizabeth	Housewife	Rochford, Essex
Guthrie, Sarah	Student	London
Hadlow, Andrew	Civil Airline Pilot	Middlesborough, Yorkshire
Hadlow, Bernadeta	Housewife	Plymouth, Cornwall
Hadow, Anne		London
Hale, Gerald	Retired	Bristol, Gloucestershire
Hale, Iris	Retired	Harrow, Middlesex
Hall, Elizabeth	Company Secretary	Sidcup, Kent
Hall, Michael	Company Director	Wimbledon, London
Hand, Angela	Legal Secretary	Kidsgrove, Staffordshire
Hand, Peter	Marketing Manager	Boscombe, Dorset
Hand, Sarah	Student	Guildford, Surrey
Harmar, David	Managing Director	Tunbridge Wells, Kent
Harmar, Jade		Eastbourne, East Sussex
Harris, Deborah	Financial Consultant	Dorking, Surrey
Harris, Martin	Manufacturer's Agent	Redhill, Surrey
Harris, Mary	Secretary/Bookkeeper	Croydon, Surrey
Hartley, Chris	Police Vehicle Builder	Crowborough, East Sussex
Hartley, Jane	Driver	Cuckfield, East Sussex
Haylock, Susan	Investment Analyst	Ilford, Essex
Hayselden, Andrew	Student	Hamilton, Bermuda

Name	Occupation	Place of Birth
Hayselden, Angela	Student	Hamilton, Bermuda
Hayselden, Patricia	Radiographer	Liverpool, Merseyside
Hayselden, Paul	Educationalist	Barnsley, Yorkshire
Hayter, Jennifer	Florist	High Hurstwood, East Sussex
Heard, David		
Heath, Jacqueline		
Heywood, Emma		Tunbridge Wells, Kent
Heywood, Jonathon	Lawyer	Watford, Hertfordshire
Heywood, Katie		Eastbourne, East Sussex
Heywood, Libby	Bursar	Esher, Surrey
Heywood, Thomas		Tunbridge Wells, Kent
Holdsworth, Brian	Retired Academic	Leeds, Yorkshire
Holdsworth, June	Retired Nurse	London
Hough, Angela	Housewife	Guildford, Surrey
Hough, Philippa	Secretary	Nassau, Bahamas
Hough, Robert	Student	Nassau, Bahamas
Hough, Timothy	Banker	Hatfield Broad Oak, Essex
Howard, Nick	Engineer	Bristol, Bristol
Howlett, Marie	Housewife	Knightsbridge, London
Howlett, Sara	Student	Cuckfield, West Sussex
Howlett, Suzanna	Student	Crowborough, East Sussex
Hryniewicz, Wanda		
Huggett, Caroline	Student	Ashford, Kent
Huggins, Jane	Personal Assistant	Heathfield, East Sussex
Huggins, Ulric		Cairo, Egypt
Huggins, Una		Sevenoaks, Kent
Hughes, Bertha	Retired	Dinnett, Aberdeenshire
Hughes, Margaretann	Accountant	Bromley, Kent
Hughes, Paul	Student	Carshalton, Surrey
Hughes, Richard	Accountant	Kingston upon Thames
Hughes, Ruth		Carshalton, Surrey
Humphry-Baker, Guy	Chartered Accountant	London
Humphry-Baker, Hannah	Student	Kingston Upon Thames
Humphry-Baker, Hilary	Teacher	Victoria, Cameroons
Humphry-Baker, Samual	Student	Kingston Upon Thames
Hyden, Susan	Management Consultant	Cannock, Staffordshire
Isaac, Betty		New Malden, Surrey
Ivey, David	Manufacturing Engineer	Reigate, Surrey
Ivey, Gary	Manufacturing Engineer	Dorking, Surrey
Ivey, Margaret	Retired	Alresford, Hampshire
Ivey, Raymond	Retired	Witley, Surrey
James, Christopher	Accountant	Brighton, East Sussex
James, Philip	Student	Pembury, Kent
James, Rebecca	Student	Pembury, Kent
James, Sheila	Office Manager	Edmonton, London
Jameson, Peter	Retired Priest	London
Johns, Barry	Retired	Southampton, Hampshire
Johns, Pamela	Retired	Perth, Perthshire
Johnson, Julie		
Johnson, Peter		

Name	Occupation	Place of Birth
Jones, David	Fund Manager	Washington DC, USA
Jones, Powell	Retired Teacher	Toronto, Canada
Kai-Whitewind, Johonaa		Leicester, Leicestershire
Kai-Whitewind, Kim	Cabinet Maker	Carshalton, Surrey
Karavias, Anthea	Student	Eastbourne, East Sussex
Karavias, Costas	Company Director	Cyprus, Cyprus
Karavias, Nadia	Student	Barking, Essex
Karavias, Stephanos	Student	Eastbourne, East Sussex
Karavias, Voula	Housewife	Cyprus, Cyprus
Keenan, Joan	Retired	London
Keenan, Kenneth	Retired	London
Keep, John	Priest	Lowestoft, Suffolk
Keiller, Quinton	Retired	Cookham Dean, Berkshire
Kelland, Rita		
Kells, Julia	Customer Services Agent	Bristol, Avon
Kells, Paula	Student	Eastbourne, East Sussex
Kells, Russ	Fireman	Eldoret, Kenya
Kells, Sian	Student	Eastbourne, East Sussex
Kiely, Mary		
Kiernan, Elizabeth	District Councillor	Penge, Kent
Kiernan, Robert	Publisher	Harrietsham, Kent
King, Christopher	Company Chairman	Uppingham, Rutland
King, Evelyn		Torquay, Devon
Lambert, Louise	Childcare	Pembury, Kent
Lambert-Dwyer, Declan		Eastbourne, East Sussex
Lampon, Jonathon	Broadcast Journalist	Gravesend, Kent
Lampon-Monk, Alasdair	Student	Brighton, East Sussex
Lampon-Monk, Amanda	Public Relations Consultant	Clapham, London
Lander, Dale	Student	Pembury, Kent
Lander, Elliott	Student	Pembury, Kent
Lander, Leigh	Airline Cabin Crew	Crowborough, East Sussex
Lander, Linda	Furnishings/Interior Designer	Crowborough, East Sussex
Lander, Nigel	Furnishings/Interior Designer	London
Langridge, Dina	Retired	Alexandria, Egypt
Langridge, Raymond	Retired	Tunbridge Wells, Kent
Lathbury, Guy	Retired	Lismore, N.S.W, Australia
Lathbury, Rosemary	Retired	St. Leonards-on-Sea, E. Sussex
Laurie, Harriet	Student	Eastbourne, East Sussex
Laurie, Ian	Project Manager	Glasgow, Strathclyde
Laurie, Maureen	Human Resources Director	Glasgow, Strathclyde
Law, Janet	Housewife/ Carer	Dorking, Surrey
Lawrence, Brian	Retired Engineer	London
Lawrence, Madeleine	Retired Psychologist	London
Lay-Flurrie, Sandra		
Lee, Emma	Bank Clerk	Eastbourne, East Sussex
Lefort, Amie	Student	Eastbourne, East Sussex
Lefort, George	Student	Eastbourne, East Sussex
Lefort, Lesley	Publican	Swindon, Wiltshire
Lefort, Paul	Publican	Rochford, Essex
Lefort, William	Student	Eastbourne, East Sussex

Name	Occupation	Place of Birth
Lenihan, Jean	Cook	Muswell Hill, London
Lenihan, Malcolm	Carpenter	Lewisham, London
Lennard, Amy	Student	Eastbourne, East Sussex
Lennard, Roberta	Civil Servant	Folkestone, Kent
Lennard, Roger	Quantity Surveyor	Worthing, West Sussex
Lenton, Mary		
Leotaud, Suzanne		
Letkeman, Sheila	Housewife	London
Lewis, Fiona	Student	Cuckfield, West Sussex
Lewis, Geraldine	Housewife	London
Lewis, Hannah	Student	Cuckfield, West Sussex
Lewis, Owen	Student	Eastbourne, East Sussex
Lewis, Peter	Electronics Engineer	Woldingham, Surrey
Livesey, Carol	Dispensing Optician	Crayford, Kent
Livesey, Juliette	Student	Derby, Derbyshire
Livesey, Richard	Company Director	Ewell, Surrey
Long, Caroline	Housewife	Wegburg, Germany
Long, Colin	Marketing	Crawley, West Sussex
Long, Frederick	Student	Pembury, Kent
Long, Harriet	Student	Pembury, Kent
Long, Imogen		Crowborough, East Sussex
Lucas, Eileen	Cattery Proprietor	Tonbridge, Kent
Lucas, Leonard	Cattery Proprietor	Murton, Co Durham
Luke, Alastair	Company Director	Bedford, Bedfordshire
Luke, Hilary	Housewife	Thames Ditton, Surrey
Luke, Michael	Trainee Manager	Crawley, West Sussex
Luke, Victoria	Student	Crawley, West Sussex
Mackay, Robert	Retired Director	Bolton, Lancashire
Maclennan, Sarah	Golf Professional	Edinburgh, Lothian
Maggs, Jacky	Secretary	Wantage, Berkshire
Mahatane, Judith	Retired Social Worker	Richmond, Surrey
Makins, Cynthia		
Mannion, Elizabeth		
Mannion, Mary		
Mansfield, Lynsay	Woodland Manager	Ilford, Essex
Mansfield, Maurice	Company Director	Headley, Hampshire
Martin, Janine	Artist	London
Martin, Richard	Writer/ Magistrate	London
Martin, Romilly	Student	London
Maskell, Sam	Kitchen Assistant	Eastbourne, East Sussex
Matthews, Deborah	Station Supervisor	Whitefield, Lancashire
Matthews, Margaret		
Mays-Smith, Alan	Charity Worker	Belmont, Surrey
Mays-Smith, Rosemary	Charity Worker	Fetcham, Surrey
McCracken, Gail	Psychotherapist	London
McCracken, Robert	Chairman of Insurance Co.	Kilmarnock, Ayrshire
McCrossan, Patrick		Croydon, Surrey
McKenzie, Michael	Lawyer	Brighton, East Sussex
McKenzie, Peggy	Housewife	London
Message, Brian	Check Out Manager	Brighton, East Sussex

Name	Occupation	Place of Birth
Middlemiss, Jennifer		
Mindell, David	Timber Broker	London
Mindell, Margaret	Retired	London
Mockridge, Susanna	Voluntary Worker	Hampstead Garden Suburb, Mddx
Monk, David	Newspaper Assistant Editor	Epsom, Surrey
Moore, Christine	Government Interviewer	Worksop, Nottinghamshire
Morris, Elizabeth	Chiropodist	Waldron, East Sussex
Morris, John	Retired	Uckfield, East Sussex
Morrison, Maureen		
Morrow, Maureen	Housewife	Hamilton, Lanarkshire
Murray, Ian	Director Software Company	Hong Kong, Hong Kong
Neal, Ernest	Retired	Eastbourne, East Sussex
Neal, Norma	Retired	Kirby-in-Ashfield, Notts
Neame, Thisbe		
Neame-Bott, Judith		
Neville, Brenda	Housewife	Ilford, Essex
Neville, Roger	Retired	
Neville, Rupert	Information Technology	Pembury, Kent
Newman, Emma	Analyst	Brighton, East Sussex
Newman, Evelyn	Clerk	Brighton, East Sussex
Newman, Richard	Police Officer	Brighton, East Sussex
Newsam, Keith	Student	Brighton, East Sussex
Newsam, Rachel	Student	Brighton, East Sussex
Newsam, Richard	Motor Mechanic	Temple Newsam, Yorkshire
Newsam, Stella	House Cleaner	Uckfield, East Sussex
Newson, Iris	Retired	Eastbourne, East Sussex
Nichols, Andrew	Retired	Rochdale, Lancashire
Nichols, Patricia	Retired	Birmingham, Warwick
Norton, Anne	Relocation Consultant	Wellington, Shropshire
Norton, Clive	Investment Banker	Llandrindod Wells, Powys
Norton, Emily	Student	London
Norton, Guy	Student	London
Norton, Kate	Student	London
Obradovits, Audrey	Cabin Crew	Wirral, Cheshire
Obradovits, Christian	Director	Salzburg, Austria
Obradovits, Oliver	Student	Brighton, Sussex
O'Sullivan, India	Student	London
Paddon, Colin	Retired	Redhill, Surrey
Parker, Donald	Retired	Smethwick, Staffordshire
Parker, June	Retired Headmistress	Wimbledon, Surrey
Parker, Margaret	Retired	Smethwick, Staffordshire
Parker, Rosalie	Archaeologist/Publisher	Chilton, Buckinghamshire
Parker-Russell, Timothy	Student	Waldron, East Sussex
Parkinson, Iris	Director	Wembley, Middlesex
Parkinson, Noel	Inventor	Armentiers, France
Parris, Bernard	Retired	Hornchurch, Essex
Parris, Ruth		Haxey, Lincolnshire
Paul, Jean	Retired	Eastbourne, East Sussex
Pearson, Antony	Driving Instructor	Farnborough, Kent
Pearson, Rita	Assistant Technical Officer	Shoreham, West Sussex

Name	Occupation	Place of Birth
Pemberton, Lorraine	Housewife	Brighton, East Sussex
Pemberton, Richard	Managing Director	Blackheath, London
Peterken, Vivienne	Astrologer	Wanstead, Essex
Petter, Donald	Software Developer	New Alresford, Hampshire
Phillips, Helen	Sales Manager	Eastbourne, East Sussex
Phillips, Martin	Company Director	Farnborough, Kent
Phillips, Oscar		Eastbourne, East Sussex
Pickett, Moyra		
Pledger, Charles		London
Pledger, Susan		London
Plowman, Mary	Housewife	Croydon, Surrey
Plowman, Peter	Senior Bank Manager	York, Yorkshire
Plowman, Robert	Student	Redhill, Surrey
Plowman, Rosemary	Student	Cambridge, Cambridgeshire
Pollock, Kathleen (Kay)	Grandmother	Edinburgh, Lothian
Porpora, Carmine	Sales Director	Hereford, Herefordshire
Porpora, Henry		Eastbourne, East Sussex
Porpora, Hugo	Student	Brighton, East Sussex
Porpora, Rupert	Student	Eastbourne, East Sussex
Porpora, Sarah	Midwife/Housewife	London
Pratt, George		
Pryer, Lee		
Pugh, Alexandra	Student	London
Pugh, Andrew	Barrister	Bexhill-on-Sea, East Sussex
Pugh, Chantal	Retired Teacher	Paris, France
Pugh, Janice	Teacher	Dulwich, London
Pugh, Norman	Dental Technician	West Norwood, London
Pugh, Sophie	Student	London
Pulham, Michael	The Christian Peace Movement	Ilford, Essex
Pulham, Patricia	Antiques/Peace Movement	Ilford, Essex
Purdey, Margaretha		Lidkoping, Sweden
Purdey, Richard	Company Chairman	Hove, East Sussex
Ransome, John	Cabinet Maker	Sidcup, Kent
Ransome, Julie	School Secretary	Bromsgrove, Worcester
Ratcliffe, Elizabeth	Housewife	Sutton, Surrey
Ratcliffe, Katherine	Student	Eastbourne, East Sussex
Ratcliffe, Suzanne	Student	Bombay, India
Ratcliffe, Timothy	Company Director	Beckenham, Kent
Ratcliffe, Timothy-James	Student	Eastbourne, East Sussex
Rayner, Joan		
Read, Deirdre	Retired	Leeds, Yorks
Read, Marian	Retailer	Lewisham, London S.E
Read, Michael	Retired	East Grinstead, West Sussex
Reader, Ann	Retired	Eygpt
Reader, William	Retired	London
Redman, John	Civil Engineer	Carshalton, Surrey
Redman, Vicki	Administrator	Glasgow, Strathclyde
Reeve, Bryan	Electronics Engineer	Chatham, Kent
Reeve, Gillian	Housewife	Maidstone, Kent
Richardson, Helen	Activity Leader	Brighton, Sussex

Name	Occupation	Place of Birth
Richardson, Ian	Duty Manager	Brighton, Sussex
Richardson, Janet	Housewife	Caterham, Surrey
Richardson, Stuart	Police Officer	North Shields, Northumberland
Ricklefs, Gerhard	Signwriter	Littlehampton, West Sussex
Rix, Anne	Teacher/Councillor	Southborough, Kent
Roberts, Jean		Cardiff, Glamorgan
Robertson, Adrian	Shop Assistant	Battersea, London
Robertson, Ruth	Secretary	Barking, Essex
Robinson, Doris	Housewife	London
Robinson, Peter	Chartered Accountant	London
Russell, Ian	University Professor	Chatham, Kent
Russell, Raymond	Publisher	Waldron, East Sussex
Rylands, Martin	Seed Potato Merchant	Weston-Super-Mare, Somerset
Rylands, Mary	Housewife	England
Sandeman, Faith		Croydon, Surrey
Sandeman, Murray	Retired	Newcastle-on-Tyne, Co Durham
Savage, Fredrika		
Savage, Trevor		
Scott, Dulce	Retired Teacher	Wilmington, Kent
Scott, Judy	Retired	London
Scott, Mason	Retired	Richmond, Surrey
Seabrook, Michelle	General Manager	Chelsea, London
Sell, Bonnie		Eastbourne, East Sussex
Sell, Chloe		Eastbourne, East Sussex
Sell, Rosemary	Retired	Knebworth, Hertfordshire
Sell, Sarah	Dental Assistant	Heathfield, East Sussex
Sell, Thomas	Computer Operator	Hackney, London
Sellick, Deborah	Teacher	Tunbridge Wells, Kent
Sellick, Jacqueline	Catering Manager	Dewsbury, Yorkshire
Sellick, William	Garden Manager	Sidcup, Kent
Seward, Jane		
Seward, Roger		
Sexton, Rosemary		
Sharpe, Ivy	Property Owner	London, Surrey
Sharpe, Peter	Property Owner	London, Middlesex
Shiers, Christine	University Lecturer, Midwifery	Enniskillen, Fermanagh
Shiers, John	Clinical Nurse Manager	Southampton, Hampshire
Simmons, Anne	Bid Manager	Sidcup, Middlesex
Simmons, Jean	Retired	St Margarets, Surrey
Simmons, Rupert	Publisher	Oldenberg, Germany
Skelton, Alexandra	Student	Eastbourne, East Sussex
Skelton, Anji	Caterer	Lewisham, London
Skelton, Robert	Metropolitan Police Officer	Chelsea, London
Slade, Joan	Retired	Essex
Slade, William	Retired	
Smart, Andrew	School Teacher	Croydon, Surrey
Smart, Lily		Tunbridge Wells, Kent
Smart, Sarah	Bank Official	Crowborough, East Sussex
Smart, Thomas		Tunbridge Wells, Kent
Smart, William		Tunbridge Wells, Kent

Name	Occupation	Place of Birth
Smith, Ann	Retired	Sevenoaks, Kent
Smith, Linda		Tenterden, Kent
Smith, Peter	Retired	Tunbridge Wells, Kent
Smith, Samantha	Student	Eastbourne, East Sussex
Smith, Terrence		Brighton, East Sussex
Soanes, Ian		
Soanes, Kalpana		
Solomons, Allen	Artist	Tampa, Fl., U.S.A
Solomons, Graham	Writer/Retired Professor	Charleston, S.C, U.S.A
Solomons, Graham	Student	Eastbourne, East Sussex
Solomons, Judith	Retired teacher	Point Pleasant, N.J, U.S.A
Soucek, Benjamin		London
Soucek, Celia	Artist/Housewife	Westerham, Kent
Soucek, Jerome	Student	Pembury, Kent
Soucek, Lucie-Anne	Student	Pembury, Kent
Soucek, Ondrej	Antiques Dealer	Prague, Czech Republic
Soucek, Quentin	Student	Farnborough, Kent
Spink, John		
Stace, Daniel	Student	Pembury, Kent
Stace, Rosemary	Technical Editor	Pembury, Kent
Steele, Dianne	Chiropodist	Stanmore, Middlesex
Sterling, Elsie	Retired	Pembury, Kent
Sterling, George	Retired	London
Stern, Gabrielle	Student	Lambeth, London
Stern, Jack	Student	Southwark, London
Stern, Rick	Chief Executive - Health Care	Camden, London
Stickland, Amanda	Teacher	Torquay, Devon
Stickland, Christopher	IT Sales	Beckenham, Kent
Stickland, Eleanor	Student	Pembury, Kent
Stickland, Madeleine		Eastbourne, East Sussex
Stickland, Sophie	Student	Pembury, Kent
Suffolk, Alan	Builder	Birmingham, West Midlands
Taylor, Emily	Student	London
Taylor, Georgia	Student	London
Taylor, Imogen	Student	London
Taylor, Karin	Photographer	London
Taylor, Steven	Insurance Broker	London
Temple, Gillian	Herb Grower/NHS Non-exec Dir.	Swindon, Wiltshire
Theis, Diane	Housewife	Harrogate, Yorkshire
Theis, Raymond	Retired	Brighton, East Sussex
Thompson, Sheila	Retired	Southampton, Hampshire
Tolley, John	Financial Consultant	Oxford, Oxfordshire
Tolley, Nancy	Housewife	Lancaster, PA., U.S.A.
Tompsett, Gloria	Housewife	Leigh, Lancashire
Tompsett, Leslie	Gardener	Lewes, East Sussex
Toomey, Dilys		
Topps, Jane	Bank Manager	Cuckfield, West Sussex
Topps, John	Pipe Fitter	Crowborough, East Sussex
Trimbee, Carol	Interior Designer	Halifax, Yorkshire
Trimbee, Olivia	Family Support Worker	Halifax, Yorkshire

Name	Occupation	Place of Birth
Trimbee, Richard	Machine Tool Engineer	Horsforth, Yorkshire
Turner, Adrian	Student	Eastbourne, East Sussex
Turner, James	Unemployed	Cuckfield, West Sussex
Turner, Joan	Housewife	Waldron, East Sussex
Turner, Kenneth	Factory Worker	Peacehaven, East Sussex
Turton, Ben	Packaging Designer	Brighton, East Sussex
Turton, Guy	Student	Cuckfield, West Sussex
Turton, Jon	Student	Brighton, East Sussex
Valentine, Charlotte	Student	Brighton, East Sussex
Valentine, Elizabeth	Veterinary Receptionist	Brighton, East Sussex
Valentine, Scott	Gardener	York, Yorkshire
Van Den Berg, Charles	Student	Kingston upon Thames, Surrey
Van Den Berg, Freddie	Student	Eastbourne, East Sussex
Van Den Berg, Lea	Reflexologist	Kuala Lumpur, Malaysia
Van Den Berg, Patrick	Student	Kingston upon Thames, Surrey
Van Den Berg, Richard	Company Director	San Jose, Costa Rica
Verco, Nancy		
Vizard, Anthony	Retired Banker	Pietermaritzburg, South Africa
Vizard, Joyce	Retired Tutor	Oxshott, Surrey
Walker, Charles	Company Director	Hereford, Herefordshire
Walker, David	Retired	Esher, Surrey
Walker, Elizabeth	Student	Poole, Dorset
Walker, Gillian	Company Director	Wokingham, Berkshire
Walker, Ian	Financial Adviser	Tunbridge Wells, Kent
Walker, Joanna	Student	Poole, Dorset
Walker, Judith	NHS Director	Birkenhead, Merseyside
Walker, Oliver	Student	Halton, Buckinghamshire
Walker, William	Student	Helensburgh, Dumbartonshire
Waller, Gabriella	Stable Manager	Pembury, Kent
Waller, Lee	Electrical Engineer	Tunbridge Wells, Kent
Waters, Karen	Casino Supervisor	Sidcup, Kent
Waters, Leslie	Retired Telecomms Engineer	Bexleyheath, Kent
Waters, Margaret	Retired Nurse	Stockwell, London
Weld, Cecily		
Weston, Lilian	Retired	Leigh, Lancashire
Westover, Paul		
White, Bryony-Beth		Crowborough, East Sussex
White, Charles		
White, Elliot		Haywards Heath, East Sussex
White, Gilean	Retired	Great Crosby, Merseyside
White, Nigel		Portsmouth, Hampshire
White, Shelley		Chichester, West Sussex
White, Yvonne		
Whitehead, Ruby	Retired	Dunblane, Central
Wickham, Dennis	Director	Blackboys, East Sussex
Wickham, Kate	Investment Accountant	Cowbeech, East Sussex
Wickham, Matthew	Student	Cowbeech, East Sussex
Wickham, Valerie	Accountant	Ringmer, East Sussex
Wilkinson, Mary	Housewife	Hayle, Cornwall
Wilkinson, Roy	Retired	Tenterden, Kent

Name	Occupation	Place of Birth
Williams, Christine	Farmer	Chorley, Lancashire
Williams, Elizabeth	Student	Eastbourne, East Sussex
Williams, Gail	Housewife	Warlingham, Surrey
Williams, Imogen	Student	London
Williams, John	Farmer	Uckfield, East Sussex
Williams, Katherine	Student	Eastbourne, East Sussex
Williams, Kenton	Farm Manager	Uckfield, East Sussex
Williams, Naomi	Housewife	Canterbury, Kent
Williams, Patricia	Development Manager	Petts Wood, Kent
Williams, Rebecca	Public Relations	Crowborough, East Sussex
Williams, Robert	Student	Pembury, Kent
Williams, Sarah	Artist	Eastbourne, East Sussex
Williams, Timothy	Surgeon	Swansea, Glamorgan
Williams-Boker, Madelein		Paderborn, Germany
Winrow, Clive		
Winterton, Anastasia		Pembury, Kent
Winterton, Beverley	Housewife	Brighton, East Sussex
Winterton, Michael	Manager	Oakham, Rutland
Woodgate, Brian		Battle, East Sussex
Woodgate, Freda	Home Carer	Woking, Surrey
Woodhouse, Lucy	Typesetter	Stratford-on-Avon, Warwickshire
Worman, Diana	Bank Worker	Bushey, Hertfordshire
Worman, Jane	Personal Assistant	Crowborough, East Sussex
Worman, Michael	Investment Consultant	Chingford, Essex

REFERENCES

Brandon, P. & Short, B, *The South East from AD1000*, Longman, 1990.

Brent, C.E., "Rural Employment and Population in Sussex Between 1550 and 1640 (part one)", *Sussex Archaeological Collections* Vol 114 pp38-48, 1976.

Brent, C.E., "Rural Employment and Population in Sussex Between 1550 and 1640 (part two)" *Sussex Archaeological Collections* Vol 116 pp41-55, 1977-78.

Brunnarius, M., *The Windmills of Sussex*, Phillimore, 1979.

Caffyn, J.M., "Sunday Schools in Sussex in the Late 18th Century", *Sussex Archaeological Collections* Vol 132 pp151-60, 1994.

Caffyn, J.M., *Sussex Schools in the Eighteenth Century*, Sussex Record Society., 1998.

Cleere, H. & Crossley, D., *The Iron Industry of the Weald*, Merton Priory Press (2nd edition), 1995.

Crossley, D., *Post-Medieval Archaeology in Britain*, Leicester University Press, 1990.

de Putron, Rev. P., *Nooks and Corners of Old Sussex*, Farncombe and Co., 1875.

Drewett, P., Rudling, D. & Gardiner, M., *The South East to AD1000*, Longman 1988.

A.C. Elliott, *The Cuckoo Line*, Wild Swan Publishing.

Foord, F., *Cross-in-Hand*, 1980.

Freemantle, A., *Three Cornered Heart*, Collins, 1971.

Gardiner, M., "The Geography and Economy of the High Weald 1300-1420" *Sussex Archaeological Collections* Vol 134 pp125-39, 1996.

Gaston, T., miscellaneous recollections (manuscript, various dates).

Gillet, Alan, and Russell, Barry K, *Around Heathfield in Old Photographs*, Alan Sutton Publishing Ltd., 1990 and 1991.

Glover, J, *Sussex Place Names*, Countryside Books., 1997.

Grantham, W.W., *Stoolball and How To Play It.*, W.B.Tattersall Ltd., 1931.

Gratwick A.S. & Whittick C., "The Loseley List of Sussex Martyrs", *Sussex Archaeological Collections* Vol 133 pp225-40, 1995.

Haslefoot, A.J., *Guide to the Industrial Archaeology of South East England: Kent, Surrey, East Sussex, West Sussex*, Batsford, 1978.

Hodgkinson, J., "The Decline of the Ordnance Trade in the Weald", *Sussex Archaeological Collections* Vol 134 pp155-67, 1996.

Holden, E.W., "A Bronze Age Loom Weight from Cross-in-Hand", *Sussex Archaeological Collections* Vol 117 1979 pp227-28 (note), 1979.

Horsfield, T.W., *The History, Antiqities and Topography of the County of Sussex,* Sussex Press, 1835.

Johnson, H.B., *Waldron's Story*, 1963.

Kelly's Directories of Sussex, Kelly Directories Ltd (various dates).

Kitchen, F., "The Ghastly War-Flame: Fire Beacons in Sussex Until the mid-17th century", *Sussex Archaeological Collections* Vol 124 pp179-91, 1986.

Ley, Rev J., "Waldron: Its Church, its Mansions, and its Manors", *Sussex Archaeological Collections* Vol 13 pp80-103.

Ley, Rev J., "Sussex Church Plate", *Sussex Archaeological Collections* Vol 55 pp216-217.

Letters from H.A. Ley to Reverand Humble-Crofts, 1906-1912 (manuscript), East Sussex Record Office PAR 499 7/7/2.

Lower, M.A., *History of Sussex*, G.P.Bacon, 1870.

Lower, M.A., "Medicinal Waters at Waldron and Mayfield", *Sussex Archaeological Collections* Vol 7 pp230-31.

McBain, F., *Waldron Parish Church and its surroundings* (pamphlet), 1985.

Mainwaring Johnston, P., "A Supposed Pre-Conquest Font at Waldron", *Sussex Archaeological Collections* Vol 49 pp126-27, 1906.

Nairn, I., *Buildings of England: Sussex*, Penguin ,1965.

National Association of Decorative and Fine Arts Societies, *Record of Church Furnishings; All Saints Waldron*, (unpublished), 1997.

Newnham, C.J., *History of the Cross in Hand Windmill and of the Newnham and Ashdown families*, East Sussex County Council Planning Department, 1979.

Nicholls, Rev L.S., Bordewich, J. & St George, C.F.L., *Waldron's Story*, (pamphlet), 1963.

Nicolson, Nigel, *Portrait of a Marriage*, Weidenfeld & Nicolson, 1973.

Pike, W.T., *Sussex in the XX Century*, Contemporary Biographies, 1910.

Rew, Henry, *Parliamentary Report on the Poultry Rearing and Fattening Industry*, H.M.S.O., 1895.

Straker, E., "A Wealden Ridgeway", *Sussex Notes and Queries* Vol pp171-73, 1936-37.

The Strand Magazine, George Newnes Ltd., 1895.

Sussex Express & County Herald, Ed., *The War in East Sussex*, 1945.

Taylor, V., Brown, R., *The Wheel of Waldron*, Heathfield & Waldron Community Association, ND.

The Victoria County History of Sussex, HMSO Vol 1-VII (various dates and authors).

Waldron Women's Institute, *Waldron Women's Institute Scrapbooks*, 1953 & 1965 (unpublished volumes, East Sussex Record Office).

Wadey, J.E., "Schools and Schooling in Sussex 1579-1686", *Sussex Notes and Queries* Vol 14 p274, 1954-57.

Waldron, Heathfield and Walberton Parish Magazine, The (various issues)

Wilson, A.E., "Sussex on the Eve of the Roman Conquest", *Sussex Archaeological Collections* Vol 93 p73, 1955.

National Monument Record, English Heritage.

Listed Building and Scheduling Descriptions, English Heritage.

INDEX

INDEX